BROKEN BONE

Ten short, off-kilter stories

Martin Crabtree

Broken Bone/ Martin Crabtree. – 2nd edition

Cover designed by CherieFox

In Memory of
Jeanne M. Benson

CONTENTS

Acknowledgments

I cannot express enough thanks to my friends for their support and encouragement. Thank you, Captain Douglas McDaniel, thank you for your personal and nautical wisdom. Thank you, Tony Reese and Brian Sarnonski for your friendship and support. To my very own Vinca Terrace friends, thank you: Mary Pastrich, Myra Batchelor, Rose Goldbach, Jim Wallenhorst, and Sherry Chapman. Not to be forgotten for their contributions are Holly Mak, Carlos and Ruby Palma, Brigitte Moore, and my wonderful Newport neighbor, Maggie Thistle. Thank you for your enthusiasm, Dr. Matthew Mahoney, Dr. Alberto Bird, and Dr. Robert Black!

Thank you for your help in researching the wonderful Dalí Museum: Sarah Fornof, Annette Norwood, and Peter Tush. To the wonderful folks out west (Lenore Harriman and others at the City of Greeley Museums Hazel E. Johnson Research Center), thanks for helping me bring Broken Bone into existence!

I also want to thank the patient souls at the Oleander Writers-Readers Connection (Five Towns) and the Dunedin Writer's Group, with a special nod to Danielle McNab. My heartfelt thanks to you all.

And to John Rehg (Soul Attitude Press): thank you for walking me through the strange world of publishing! You are patience personified.

Read Me First

I *thought* I heard the people behind me on the airplane mention a place called Broken Bone, but I looked it up when I landed and there doesn't seem to be such a place. So, if strangers can make up a place while sitting in a thin metal tub that flies through the air, I can—and did—too.

The stories in this book are about people that somehow connect to Broken Bone. As you read along, don't worry about Sheila's big words; she doesn't. It would help, too, if you believe that Kevin can fly.

But most of all, I hope you enjoy these stories; most are pretty happy. Sometimes not, though. Who knows what you get when you peel the skin off a balloon?

Anyways, the only way out of this oubliette is UP! (A note from Sheila: an oubliette is a prison cell with a trap door in the top as its only way in, or out.)

Characters

Here's a list of characters that may help as you read through these stories. They are not in order of appearance but, instead, are listed by how they are related.

Dr. Zachary Ritenour. Pioneering obstetrician who, in 1872, finds himself way out west. Pity he can't tell clouds from mountaintops.

Octavia. A native New Yorker, she spent time among the Ute's, learning their ways. Her knowledge of the land, and birthing babies, proves invaluable to Dr. Ritenour.

Mrs. Trudy Tremolo. Landlady who rents lodgings in Sawnick, Colorado to Dr. Ritenour. She's plain and plainspoken, and also rents out donkeys.

Margaret and **Alma (donkeys)**. They're donkeys. Enough said! Mrs. Tremolo calls them *kitsaan*—no good, bad, ruined. And they are really really really miserable cusses.

Mr. and Mrs. Gipson. Residents of Greeley Colony, a social experiment that has its shortcomings—including doctors that are not up on the newest field of medicine, obstetrics. Pity, given that Mrs. Gipson is about to give birth;

Mr. Gipson, always impatient, just can't wait. She wrote to Dr. Ritenour and begged him to help her when the time comes. And it does.

Mrs. Sheila Fitzgerald Short. Sheila has loved big words, no doubt about it, ever since she was a young girl in Dorchester, Massachusetts. She grew up, married her childhood friend, Jameson Short, and had a precocious son (See: Dickie Short). Fond of unusual cocktails, unusual clothing, and Virginia Woolf, she makes her way to Washington, DC and her "salubrious" adventures begin.

Celeste Lobosco. Celeste grew up in Dorchester with Sheila, but confesses that even she is sometimes baffled by Sheila's vocabulary. As retirement arrives, she cheers Sheila on to join her (and Celeste's husband, Joseph) in St. Petersburg, Florida. Celeste enjoys having cocktails with her feisty upstairs neighbor (See: Victoria Welden), but senses all is not happy in that household.

Dickie Short. Ten year old Dickie—full name Richard—wants to be just like everyone else, but feels his eccentric mother (See: Sheila Short) is somehow holding him back.

Kevin D'Arcangelo. Kevin is Dickie's first friend in his new home of Washington, DC. And Kevin seems to be everything Dickie is not: sure of himself. Together, they discover the secret to flying.

Marshall O'Malley. Small-town boy Marshall left Broken Bone to see all the sights that Boulder, Colorado has to offer. Life is a *goat rope*, he thinks. Forty seems about the right age to grow up, and out, right? Lucky for him, he meets Sandro (See: Sandro D'Arcangelo) who proves to be a good life coach.

Alessandro "Sandro" D'Arcangelo. Big-city boy Sandro, fresh from DC, feels right at home in Boulder,

Colorado, and even in small-town Broken Bone. With a wink, and a hearty laugh, he helps Marshall—and maybe even Marshall's family—relax and *enjoy* the goat rope that is life. Please note that Sandro is Kevin D'Arcangelo's cousin.

Jake, Lydia, and Aria O'Malley. The O'Malley's are pillars of the Broken Bone community. Jake is a hard working, conservative man who raised his younger brother (Marshall) after their parents died. Lydia has a heart full of love, and hands full of her adolescent daughter (Aria) and Dotty (Lydia's mother). Aria is at the crush-and-blush stage and *really likes* meeting Sandro, and Dotty's stroke leaves her likely to say just anything.

Randa D'Arcangelo. Kevin's wife, Randa, just *can't* decide how best to decorate—re-decorate, really—her home. She's a gifted linguist disguised as Audrey Hepburn, with an inclination to indulge in strange new religions. She knows how to make the best of her gifts.

Mr. Bartholomew ("Barry") Youngston Simmons. A self-made millionaire, this Texan falls hard for his neighbor, Sheila Short. When all seems lost for the seniors in Vinca Terrace, he puts his head together with a smart-as-a-whip lawyer (See: Russian Reeves, Esq.) to see how he can help.

Russian ("Russ") Reeves, Esq. He's an attorney-at-law—that means he's a lawyer. Russ is dedicated to helping his clients, especially when they're up against the big bad guys. Just ask Barry Simmons.

Ms. Tiffany Rebecca Ursula Mercedes Palma (T.R.U.M.P.). Tiffany is a young, thirtyish woman who goes her own way, you hear what we're sayin'? She makes hats out of recycled materials, finds and loses jobs—regularly. She's a little lost, a little found. Oh, and she's the niece of Victoria Weldon.

Mrs. Victoria Welden. Victor is a firecracker, born and reared in Broken Bone. She moves to St. Petersburg, Florida, to marry a highly-decorated man (See; Neal Welden). Mistakes happen, yes?

Mr. Neal Weldon. Picture an oaf. With *lots* of tattoos. Redeeming virtues? Well, he does love dogs. He should put out that cigar, be nicer to his wife (See: Victoria Welden), and definitely avoid high places!

Ms. Eloise Tristler. She lives in Broken Bone, Colorado (a place that's as real as Vinca Terrace), works for a decorating firm (Homes Again), yearns to be Broken Bone's first woman mayor ever since she flunked her audition at Julliard School of Music. Oh, and she's "into" inventing a new religion.

Ms. Angie Sparks. Angie has become Sheila's good friend and confidant at the Quebec House. When she gets brutally "let go" by an evil law firm because she (gasp!) grew older, Sheila is determined to set things right. But some things are beyond even the power of the determined Sheila Short!

Ms. Clara Davies. One day, she fell off her platform shoes (again), ruined her shoulder, and had to close her shop (Arch Friends). She can't say enough good things about her "little helper", Tiffany (See: Tiffany Rebecca Ursula Mercedes Palma), who was mixed up with a roofer and now makes hats at the mall.

Ms. Arlene Tyler. Arlene is the Welcome Lady for Vinca Terrace. Best to talk to her in person, at least until she gets those new hearing aids she's been talking about—for years.

Ms. Peg from Vinca 426. Peg rides a mean scooter along the walkways of Vinca Terrace, tooting its horn and trying very hard not to tip it over when she's scooting around in her

Vinca Terrace home. Tipping over is bad, very bad, and she'll tell you that because she's done it so many times before.

Broken Bone

Sawnick, Colorado Territory,
Mid-April, 1872

"By donkey, Sawnick to Greeley Colony's a full day's ride," Mrs. Trudy Tremolo told her lodger. Dr. Zachary Ritenour stood in front of his rooming house with his short, ample landlady. They were inspecting her two donkeys tied to the hitching post in the street that ran along Sawnick's main, only, dusty road.

"Mrs. Tremolo," said Dr. Ritenour, "they need me urgently in the Greeley Colony. I'm a stranger in this part of the world, and it is not at all like Boston. Riding the train here is one thing, and riding horses, but I don't know where to begin with these odd looking animals, much less how to get there."

"It's an easy ride, Doc. Just sit, the donkey knows the way. Greeley Colony's yonder that way," she said, pointing toward the rising sun. "Keep the mountains behind you and you'll be goin' in the right direction. Comin' back, of course, do it 'tother ways around. And don't worry none about Alma, that donkey can find her way home in fire or flood, even I reckon a passel of snakes.

"Got her and her stupid cuss of a sidekick here from one'a them Ute Indians. Told me they were kitsaan, been told that means no good, bad, ruined. Yup, told me they was tizipe. Even I know that means evil. Said they found 'em in that place, in that place between Jackson and Camp Bell. Ute's call it Hell on Earth in their Indian-talk, must'a been pretty bad if they didn't like it."

She clucked at the animal to get her attention with no results. "I'd say take Margaret here, she's a bit easier for a tenderfoot, but lately she's been runnin' round in circles, goin' nowheres fast, her long ears floppin' real funny. But both them asses can kiss my pants!" Mrs. Tremolo rose on her toes—her long skirt a dull bell, her small feet dusty clappers—and leaned over the hitching rail; she spit snuff with gusto into the dry road. She continued, her voice thick with phlegm.

"And 'nother thing," she said, "don't talk too much 'bout bein' from Sawnick. Far as they think, this here town is chock full of runaways from Greeley. Who could blame 'em, for runnin' away I mean, what with no drinkin' or fleshpots, haventa dig water ditches, and who knows what. Put up a big ole fence 'round the whole place, too. Old man Greeley came out ta see what he started, 'bout two years back, but—" she spat again, "he turned right around and lit outta here and ain't been seen 'round here since."

Zachary Ritenour stood beside the stinking animals and clutched his saddle bag of medical supplies. "Thank you for your help, Mrs. Tremolo. I should be glad they called me over to Greeley to deliver the baby. Most folks don't trust doctors to deliver babies, I guess I should thank Mrs. Gipson for insisting on me. Especially a doctor who believes Dr. Semmelweis is right, good hygiene can prevent childbed fever. Maybe this will encourage others, so I won't have to go back to Boston."

She helped the doctor onto his mount, check his saddlebag, and gave the animal's rump a good slap. "Name the kid after me, how's about? Just don't give him the donkey's name, we sure don't need 'nother Alma! Or, God help us, Margaret!" Mrs. Tremolo stood on the unpainted porch and watched the tall, thin man ride slowly eastward. She could hear him repeating her advice about keeping his back to the mountains. Turning back in to her rooming house, she muttered "Kick her real hard, doc, she needs it. Who knows, maybe she likes it?"

*   *   *   *   *

The Greeley Colony

The rising sun was a red arrow in Dr. Ritenour's open eyes, a red blot when he closed his eyes. Alma juddered along the earthy path, stopping often to paw the flat dirt, nibble, and nudge rocks. "Hate to do this to you," Dr. Ritenour said the first time he kicked her. "Sorry," he said the second time, with more feeling in his feet than in his words. He offered no further apologies as he urged her along the way to Greeley Colony.

"So here I am," he said aloud to the world too far away to hear him. "Feeling like Don Quixote abandoned by Sancho Panza. I might look a little like him, but you, donkey, are the size and shape of mortal sin." Alma stopped to nudge more rocks as he spoke. "Another kick start, eh, my stubborn doongi." The donkey snorted at his last word. "Oh, yes, I heard Mrs. Tremolo call you that, it must be Ute for donkey, yes?" An extra hard kick, and they were on their way again.

The day drummed Dr. Ritenour's senses into a new awareness. The sun spun, the mountains slid behind the thin doctor and the fat ass. The wind insinuated, hissed rumors, never spoke directly. Man and beast were a weary dot and dash, each moment more punishing for the tenderfoot.

When the sun touched the Rockies behind them, Zachary Ritenour stopped and squinted at the flat landscape in front of them. "I think that's it, don't you doongi?" he asked, with no response. He repeated the question, using both feet.

As they rode closer, he saw the wire fence around the Colony. "Prickly wire fence runs clear 'round the whole place," Mrs. Tremolo said earlier, "said it was to keep cows outta their gardens. Just 'bout seven feet high, nearly fifty miles long, and the fence ain't finished yet. Even put up two gates, so's they can lock 'em tight from spring to fall. Donkey'll know where to find the gate."

Alma earned her keep and took Dr. Ritenour to the western gate; it was open. A large sign painted on the wire fence beside the gate said "Welcome to Union Colony. Population: 1,000 souls. Enter here all who believe in Faith, Family, Education, Irrigation, Temperance, Agriculture, and Home."

"I would be hard pressed to argue with that," Dr. Ritenour told Alma. "Though the Temperance might chafe." He pulled a letter out of his saddlebag, the letter from Mrs. Lina West Gipson asking him to come to Greeley. "You'll know our home instantly," Mrs. Gipson wrote. "It is quite square, surrounded by a wide front porch, deep blue trim, and two prominent bay windows. Four large columns hold up a pediment with Greek and Roman figures. Quite garish by the Colony's standards, but in keeping with my husband's fondness for Italian architecture."

She enclosed a hand-drawn map of Greeley Colony. "Come on now, doongi, I know the way from here." He used kicks and the reins to make his way over and across the grid of Greeley's streets. Dr. Ritenour stopped in front of a large white home with the name A.E. Gipson above its doorway. But he didn't need a map or a description or a sign in front of the house: Mrs. Lina West Gipson's screams, a thrilling contralto of pain, could be heard throughout the Union Colony.

Dr. Ritenour threw Alma's reins over the hitching post, grabbed his saddlebag and bounded up the front walk. At his first sharp knock on the ornate door, it swung open. "Doctor, come in. Quickly!" said a tall, balding man with big ears, and extended his hand. "Albert Gipson. Wife's this way. Follow me." Before they could shake hands, Mr. Gipson grabbed Dr. Ritenour's elbow and led him up the heavily carpeted stairs in the front hall. "First door on the left," he said. Richer, deeper, longer screams confirmed his directions.

Dr. Ritenour leaned against the balustrade at the top of the stairs. "Mr. Gipson, I will need all the fresh linen you have, a large basin of boiling water, and some strong soap. Quickly, please!" Dr. Ritenour knocked once, opened the bedroom door, and began to earn his keep.

*   *   *   *   *

Dr. Ritenour nearly tripped on the layers of oriental rugs scattered inside the doorway to Mrs. Gipson's bedroom. The room was dimly lit, the curtains drawn against the setting sun and the early Spring chill. The only light came from the fireplace in the corner. In a large brass bed, the sweat-drenched blonde curls of a woman's head tossed back and forth among a fort of pillows. "Doctor, doctor, doctor," she moaned.

"Here, Mrs. Gipson. I left Boston and came as quickly as I could, although your letter made me think you would not be ready for several more weeks." He opened his saddlebag and spread out his medical instruments on the trunk at the foot of the bed.

"Do you have the Twilight Sleep I wrote to you about? Please, please, I'm in such pain!"

"Mrs. Gipson," he said, reaching for her hand. He checked her pulse, felt her forehead, and lightly touched her through the sweat-soaked sheets. "Mrs. Gipson, I would not advise any medication. Twilight Sleep may help you with pain, or even forget the pain, but it is made from morphine and scopolamine which I don't—"

From out of the shadows, a young woman stepped beside Dr. Ritenour and touched his hand; he pulled back in surprise. He felt warm where her flesh touched his. He thought the fire burned brighter.

"Doctor, I hope you do not think she should, as they say, bring forth children in sorrow!"

He pulled himself up to his full height, and took his measure of the woman in front of him. She is not exactly pretty, I believe a writer would call her handsome. He flushed. Before he could speak, she said softly, "I'm afraid it's my fault. I misjudged her time. And I'm sorry to have startled you. I'm Octavia, Mrs. Gipson's assistant." She looked directly at him with clear gray eyes and held out a hand to him. They were evenly matched for height.

Dr. Ritenour was still for a few moments, then gave her a small bow. He did not take her hand. "No, no, not at all, it's just that—"

"Perhaps you believe that the pain will make her love her child more, and that childbirth is a noble feat?" Octavia placed her refused hand on her hip, the other hand rested on the lace collar around her neck. Her voice was slightly sharper. She arched an eyebrow.

"No," the doctor said again, and turned toward his patient. "Mrs. Gipson, you seem to be in more pain than I would expect this early. The pain medicine would make it difficult for you to speak, and difficult to push. It may be necessary for me to use forceps, or even to perform a Cesarean section."

Mrs. Gipson moaned louder, her fists pulling hard on the linen sheets. Dr. Ritenour turned back to Octavia.

"Babies born to heavily medicated women can be very sleepy and have to fight hard to breathe. They often need resuscitation." He stepped around her to reach his medical supplies; Octavia touched his hand again as he passed her, and again he felt the same strong warmth. Perhaps, he thought, the long journey with little food and water is making me giddy. This handsome woman is magnetic. But I must focus on my patient...

"In that case, Doctor, I will make her my special tea. I was just about to do that when I heard you arrive."

"May I trouble you for some tea, too? It's been a very long journey."

Octavia laughed. "I don't think you'd care too much for this tea, doctor. It's for healing. I make it from bear root and the bark of ponderosa pine. An old Ute secret. But I will make you some of my special three leaf sumac tea, that should revive you." She was out the door before he could reply.

"Trust her, doctor," said Mrs. Gipson, her voice husky. "Trust her."

The doctor pulled up a chair beside the bed, facing Mrs. Gipson. "She's a very unusual woman, isn't she?" He mopped her forehead with a compress from the basin beside the bed. "Very unusual."

Mrs. Gipson grimaced from a new wave of pain, then relaxed as it subsided. "She's spent quite a bit of time among the Utes, learning their ways so she could teach them ours. She came out here with us two years ago. I think—" she stopped to breathe deeply, then continued, "—I think she's become more like them than she is like us. Though she comes from a very fine New York family."

"Mrs. Gipson, rest as much as you can now. Your husband will be in shortly with some supplies, and with God's help—"

"—and Octavia's" whispered Mrs. Gipson.

"—we'll bring your first born into this world. Mother and child will be fine, I've done this many times before." He mopped her forehead again and settled in for a long evening.

* * * * *

Twenty-three hours later

Dr. Ritenour staggered down the stairs and nearly fell into the parlor. Mr. Gipson was asleep in a wing chair by the fire; the doctor folded himself into a corner of the couch beside the chair. He called Mr. Gipson's name until he started out of his slumber.

"What? What??" He blinked and stretched, then saw the doctor. "How is she? I must know immediately!" He grabbed the chair's arms and pulled himself to his feet.

"Mr. Gipson, she's fine, fine," said Dr. Ritenour. His voice was weak, he did not rouse from his position. "Fine, indeed. Mother and children are fine." He tried to sink down into the couch to get some sleep.

"Mother and ... did you say children?" The doctor did not reply. "Children?! Doctor?"

"Yes, Mr. Gipson, two fine young men. Twins, to be precise, born nearly forty-five minutes apart. Your wife is amazingly strong. Healthy, each of them. Twins often come early." The doctor roused himself and stood beside the fire, one hand balancing on the mantle. He looked around the living room with dull astonishment. Mrs. Gipson's letter only hinted at the frenzy of Italian furnishings: a clutter of ferns on pedestals, a pair of brocade footstools, a rococo room screen, a pair of overstuffed couches, and a large statue in the corner of Venus de Milo. From the center of the ceiling hung a chandelier that, even unlit, sent light flying around the room. An ebony Forneaux Pianista, ready to play tunes from its folding cards, was visible in the adjacent room. Can it be a lack of sleep, or is this room in entirely the wrong place? Dr. Ritenour wondered. And who is that strange woman, Octavia? Her tea is a miracle. Made a very long delivery one of the easiest. Must ask Octavia... his knees buckled, he slid toward the floor, but caught himself on the mantle.

Mr. Gipson grabbed him under his arms and steered him back to the couch. "Sit there for a few minutes, Doctor. I'll have Octavia bring you some refreshments." Mr. Gipson almost danced out of the room and up the stairs, calling Octavia and his wife as he went.

Sitting on the edge of the couch, Dr. Ritenour drifted in and out of sleep for several minutes until he heard his name being called.

"Dr. Ritenour, here, sit back and drink this. It's some wild onion soup, and I've brought you some warm chokecherry wine. My own recipe." Octavia helped him settle back, and arranged the soup and wine on the table beside him. "Looks like heavy weather out there," she said, pulling the velvet curtains back from one of the windows. "Heavy weather." She sat in the chair where Mr. Gipson spent the previous night.

Dr. Ritenour devoured his soup and wine quickly. They sat in silence for a few minutes, then he stood up and looked out the window. "In Boston, I'd say those are snow clouds. The clouds look like ironclad warships, some would say. They look far away, but I better leave before the storm starts."

"You are correct, Doctor. But you are in no shape for your trip back. I suggest you rest before you head for home. And Alma may not take kindly to another trip so soon."

Dr. Ritenour stood at the window for a quiet minute. He turned and looked at Octavia, the pearly light on her face giving her a satin glow. "Octavia, I ... must. I must return, or risk getting caught in the storm or worse." He paused, and looked out the window as he spoke. "I just don't know .... You were really ..." He fell silent, and returned to the couch.

Octavia stood slowly, smoothing her long, wrinkled skirt. "I think I understand, Doctor." A smile, a sigh. She held out upturned palms toward him, as if to say that words are not enough. "Let me help you get ready for your trip back." He held out his hands so she could help him off the couch.

"Doctor, before you leave, will you please look at my hands? They feel curiously warm..."

*   *   *   *   *

The Ride Back

The snow spun, the mountains slipped away. Heavy clouds disguised themselves as snowy mountain tops. Dr. Ritenour was exhausted and lost. He knew it, and kicked Alma repeatedly as if it were her penance.

"Devil, devil!!" he cried as Alma stumbled on a rock and threw him to the ground. His foot twisted as he broke his fall. "Beast!" he yelled again, but she was gone, gone along with his saddlebag and part of his sanity.

He didn't need his degree from Harvard Medical School to know he had a broken foot. "It's only a fracture of the base of the fifth metatarsal," he said aloud to the world too far away to hear him. "Ankle rolls inward, fragment of the bone is pulled off by peroneus tendon. Often heals nicely with conservative care—no operation is needed. At least, that's what they told us in medical school."

The snow fell against the earth, against more snow, against the doctor.

Dr. Ritenour pushed through the storm, ignoring his injured foot. He shouted into the wind for his beast, letting snow and cold fly in. He shouted for the donkey long gone. He shouted his despair. "Why couldn't Mrs. Gipson have had just one child? Or been quicker if she had to have twins?"

He stumbled, he fell, delirious, angry, hopeless. On the ground, the snow felt warm, it was heavenly-clean linen, it spoke of sleep. Dr. Zachary Ritenour slid into unconsciousness.

* * * * *

Another Birth

The air was warm and fragrant, and Dr. Ritenour woke refreshed. And confused. The ground beneath him was damp, and he could see the grass. There was a light dusting of snow, but the deep snow was gone.

He sat up, squinting against the rising sun. He stood. He saw two cloth sacks near where he had slept, and a leather water bag. A few feet away, a fire burned with a small pot suspended above it; steam rose from the pot. Beyond the fire, he heard running water and saw a small creek nearby.

He walked to the creek, knelt, and drank deeply. From the corner of his eye, he saw movement in a stand of trees. He stood to turn—though he did not know where to go. He heard a woman singing, a clear soprano. He squinted at the woods in front of him: It was Octavia. "In the sweet by and by, We shall meet on that beautiful shore."

"Ahoy!" the doctor shouted, at a loss for a more appropriate greeting in his particular circumstance. "Ahoy!"

"Ahoy back, Doctor!" Octavia sang to the same tune, "Ahoy back." Within moments she was standing beside him. Her chestnut hair was free of its earlier restraints and cascaded around her shoulders. Gone was her modest lace blouse and long, soft skirt. She wore a buckskin dress decorated with intricate quillwork in vivid black, yellow, and red. Leggings and moccasins took the place of the shoes and stockings she wore in the Greeley Colony. She held a large pointed stick in her right hand, and several plants in her left hand.

"Before you ask, I shall tell you what I imagine you want to know." She handed him the plants and led him by the elbow, not needing to kick or cuss.

The doctor stood by the fire; she took back the plants, ripped them apart, and put them in the steaming pot. "I was certain you would get lost. I've seen Alma in action," she said before he could comment. "She's devious, she's tizipe. Evil. Besides, Mr. Gipson is suddenly a very attentive husband, now that he has two heirs. One would have thrilled him, and he believes this miracle is somehow your doing. So Mrs. Gipson will be fine in his care for quite a while."

"But, really—"

"Please be patient, Doctor," she said and laughed at her own joke. She touched his hand again, and he felt the familiar warmth. "When I saw how bad the storm was, I simply followed you. These are the clothes I wore when I lived with the Utes."

"How—"

"Now, Doctor, why do you always, never ... please. I learned much from my time with the Utes, they are really brilliant. Besides, we're not much more than an hour's walk from the Colony. And, Doctor, how is your foot?"

Dr. Ritenour gasped. He had forgotten his broken bone completely! "Now, Octavia," he said, and sat on a large rock nearby, "you can't tell me that the miracle tea you gave me—"

"No, not at all, Doctor. No tea. It was a compress, just like that you used on Mrs. Gipson. I told you the Utes are brilliant! They use bear root for indigestion, infections, and even wounds."

The doctor squinted in disbelief, as if that could establish his credentials with her. He stood quickly, then looked at his foot. "By all that is holy, you don't think..."

"No, doctor, I don't. But I DO think YOU think you broke your foot. When I found you, you were muttering broken bone over and over. I think," she said, and gave him a sunny smile, "I think you simply hurt or bruised it, and that the compress eased the pain." She sat on the rock beside him. He felt her warmth through her deer-hide dress.

"And the snow, the cold, surely the Utes cannot..."

"Yes and no," she continued, "by the time I found you, a Chinook wind had come up. They warm up the coldest winter days in just a few hours, they can even melt snow. As you can see," she said, looking around. "I got a fire going, and used my digging stick here"—she banged the ground with the long sturdy stick, and showed him its sharp point —"to get you some nice healing medicine."

Before he could respond, she leaned into him, unmistakably into him, and said, "If we're going back, or on to Sawnick, we should leave now. It won't stay warm long."

"But I ... I... did you say IF?"

"Well, yes, yes I did." She got up to stir the pot. "But I have a better idea."

Dr. Ritenour sighed. "I am afraid to ask. But I believe you will tell me regardless."

"While you were sleeping—"

"I was unconscious, nearly in a coma, been awake for many hours..."

"While you were sleeping, I had a few ideas. I think we both think things can be better. Yes?"

"Yes."

"Greeley Colony is not much of a utopia. Places like Sawnick will come and go, once the thrill of being able to drink and gamble again wear off." She got a metal cup from the cloth sack, poured hot liquid from the pot into it and offered it to him.

"Hmm... interesting," he said.

"Which? What I said, or the soup?"

"Both. Pray continue."

"So," and she drew a deep breath, gray eyes locked onto his brown eyes, "let's start our own place. One that gives respect to the Utes and to everyone else. One that has guiding principles, but is not a prison. One that does not drug women."

"Yes, but—"

"Doctor, you always never let me finish. And, and, ... let's call it Broken Bone." She gave him a pleased-with-herself smile. "Not," she added, "because of your foot, but we will break tradition, down to the bone."

She continued her song where she left off, and the doctor joined her in harmony, singing aloud to each other, close enough for just the two of them to hear. "In the sweet by and by, We shall meet on that beautiful shore . . ."

*   *   *   *   *

Mrs. Tremolo looked up from her sewing when she heard a familiar snort outside the parlor of her rooming house. She hurried outside, and held up a hand against the blowing snow. A dark form stood in front of her porch. It was Alma: braying insinuations, hissing rumors, never speaking directly. "Well, it's about gol dang time you got here!" Mrs. Tremolo pulled the donkey by her reins and dragged her into the shed behind the rooming house. "There!" she yelled into the donkey's ears, "there's water, and over there's food. Drink, eat, you fool." She gave the donkey's rump a slap and returned to her parlor.

She started to pick up her sewing, but hesitated. Aloud, to the world too far away to hear her, she said, "Must be gettin' soft in the head, seems I'm forgettin' somethin' or somebody, but don't rightly recollect what it is. That damn Alma!"

Vocabulary

Dorchester, Massachusetts,
Fall of 1938

"I think you'll like this, Terry." Sheila Fitzgerald whispered to her sister so she wouldn't disturb the other library patrons. "It's a very long book, with *lots* of big words!" She pushed her glasses against the bridge of her nose and settled down to read. "Call me Ishmael…"

Sheila read softly, losing herself in the story, her ten-year old voice soft and high, hardly ever struggling with the big words. But she stopped and sniffed: something smelled like church, something different, something not a library smell. She looked around to see what was wrong.

The radiator behind them steamed their wet wool mittens. "Oh no, Terry!" Sheila whispered as loud as she dared. "Mittens don't go on radiators. Ma won't understand. We can't burn down the library!" Sheila leaned back in her chair and pulled the mittens by their strings. Her sister did not stir.

A sudden beam of sunlight from a high window caught Terry's copper hair; Sheila looked up and thought it made it her sister look like one of the pictures in her religion book, one of the pictures of pious saints with the Paraclete Tongues of Flame. Sheila loved learning new words, even if Sister Stella Maris' vocabulary lessons were very strict.

Sheila started reading again. Terry moved her head in and out of the sunbeam, playing with light and shadows on the inside of her eyelids. Their corner of the Dorchester Public Library glowed. Muffled traffic rolled by on Neponset Avenue outside, like the waves at nearby Tenean Beach;

both girls grew sleepy. It was a perfect afternoon in Dorchester, cuddled up against Boston. Dorchester was in its middle-aged glory. The world was at peace, and the early fall of 1938 was especially crisp and dry.

Long before the girls met Captain Ahab it was time to go. The sunbeam faded and Sheila could feel the cool October air seeping through the library walls.

"Come on, Terry, *wake up!*" Sheila said and snapped the book shut. "You can sleep anywhere, can't you?" She helped her sister with her coat, scarf, mittens, and hat.

As the girls left the library, they waved to the brownstone across the street. Terry cupped her mittened hands and yelled, "Hello, Aunt May! Hello, Uncle Joe!" There was no sign of life behind the curtains Aunt May had crocheted from kite string.

Sheila turned and quietly said, "Tooda-loo, Library!"

On the way home they waved to the house where Aunt Shirley and Uncle Al lived, Pope's Hill where Aunt Sadie lived, and waved to Mrs. Quinlovan on her way to a Novena. No one was a stranger in Dorchester.

Heady smells of corned beef and cabbage perfumed Neponset Avenue. Early evening traffic hummed beside them. Trolleys rang bells and truck tires sang. For two blocks Sheila had to pull at Terry's elbow half a dozen times; she liked to stop to pet dogs and chuck them under their chins. They listened to her slow speech, wagging their tails and drooling over their enormous teeth.

"Come *on*, Theresa Louise. If we're late, Ma will be *truculent!*" Terry was twelve—almost two years older—but Sheila knew her sister wouldn't understand the new vocabulary word. Terry was *retarded.*

Sheila learned that word last year from Sister Stella Maris. It was a few days after the fifth grade took the *Revised Stanford-Binet Intelligence Test* that Sister asked Sheila to have her mother come by after school. Sheila waited at her desk while Sister spoke with Mrs. Fitzgerald in the hallway. Through the wavy glass of the classroom door, Sheila could see the figure of Sister wiggle as she crossed herself. The nun's sharp voice resonated down the hallway and Sheila heard her say *But God gave you one who is so bright. We really should have skipped her another two grades.* Sister's voice dropped, and Sheila knew this must be about Terry. The nun said something less distinct, something about *retarded* and *has an IQ of less than 70.* Mrs. Fitzgerald did not move, and Sheila could not hear her speak. Ever since then, St. Ann's School let Terry sit in the back of the classroom and look out the window; she did not have to answer Sister's strict questions.

Retarded! thought Sheila as she walked along Neponset Avenue. *That doesn't tell you how beautiful and sweet she is.* The sun flamed cherry red and the wind was picking up.

When the girls turned onto Southwick Street, Sheila grabbed Terry's hand and ran down the short hill to their brownstone. Together the girls pushed open the front door of Number Eight. The lace curtain on the door's oval window fanned out across the wallpaper's faded roses.

"Ma! We're home!!" "We're home!" echoed Terry, beaming. The girls pulled off their mittens and hats and dropped them on the hallway table.

Mrs. Fitzgerald came out of the kitchen, wiping her hands on her flowered apron, her face a ruddy rose from the stove and gin. "Which of you girls left that wagon in the parlor?" she demanded. "Sheila?" Her voice blended first-generation Boston and Brogue.

Sheila stamped her foot. "But ma, why do you *always* think it's *me*? Terry could have—"

"Never mind about Terry." Mrs. Fitzgerald steered Sheila's thin shoulders toward the wagon in the front room. "Just put the wagon on the back porch. You'll be needing it in the morning. Tomorrow's Commodities Day. Now there's a good girl."

Sheila gave a little groan. Every Thursday morning before school, she and Terry took the wagon to Maggie's Dry Goods on Pope's Hill to get their share of Commodities for the Needy. They filled the wagon with tin cans donated by more affluent neighbors; Sheila thought they gave only what they didn't like.

"Then I want you both to wash up for supper. Terry, you get to set the table tonight." Mrs. Fitzgerald returned to the kitchen, back to her drink and dinner preparations.

"Did you hear that, Sheila? I get to set the table tonight, I get to set the table tonight" Terry sing-songed as she followed her sister to the back porch. She was beaming.

"Yes, sweetie," Sheila said absently. She dropped the wagon's handle on the painted wood floor beside the piles of laundry Mrs. Fitzgerald washed for her neighbors—those that could find work. The stacks of clothing nearly filled the back porch, completely hiding the wicker couch that used to live in their house on Cape Cod. Clothes lines criss-crossed the small room; empty overalls and cotton dresses dangled like abandoned bodies. A wool coat was draped across the oil heater that made the room smell like church.

Sheila picked up a small rubber ball and several shiny metal stars and held them out to her sister. "Jacks?" she asked.

"Yes!" Terry loved to play jacks. She said, in her slow, happy way as she always did, "I could play this *forever!*" Terry never missed, and Sheila usually grew quite bored. Sheila spent most of their games fetching the ball when it got away from her. Sometimes she regretted having taught her sister the game. Tonight, though, Sheila thought her sister looked like an angel and could refuse her nothing.

The girls collapsed onto the floor and played until Mrs. Fitzgerald called them to supper.

* * * * *

"Sheila. *Sheila.* Wake up, for the love of Pete." Mrs. Fitzgerald shook her daughter's feet beneath the worn Chenille bedspread. Sheila woke to see her mother's figure breaking the line of light from the hallway; the bedroom door was open just a sliver.

"What? What?" Sheila asked. "What time is it?"

"It's Thursday, that's what time it is. Don't wake your sister, though. She isn't feeling well today. I'm surprised you didn't hear her crying last night. You'll have to go alone. Dress warm, it's blessed cold outside this morning."

Sheila got up mechanically and started to dress. Thursday, she thought. On Tuesday it's dairy from St. Ann's, and Thursday it's Commodities for the Needy. I wish I didn't know what commodities meant. I'll bet rich people don't have to get their food in a wagon. And we wouldn't be so poor if... She looked at her sister, immobile under her blankets, a scarlet string of hair on the pillow. I wonder what she thought when Daddy died. I'm sure that's why she cries.

Last summer had seemed kind, sunnier than most Dorchester summers. Right after Mass at St. Ann's, the whole family and two uncles walked the half mile to Tenean Beach with their bathing suits under their clothes, their beach shoes the only outward sign of their destination. Sheila's father made both his daughters stop and look as they crossed the tracks of the railroad where he worked. "You can't be too careful," Tommy Fitzgerald said.

The girls left Uncle Patrick and Uncle Sean on the beach—Tenean was mostly rocks and cold water—to talk about their new jobs at the fire station and other adult things with Sheila's mother. Tommy played in the sparkling water with his children.

"Ma!" Sheila called from the water, "Uncle Pat! Look at Daddy. See how he can float!" Sheila and Terry clapped their hands, their father face down in the water.

At the wake, Terry kept asking her sister what *condolences* meant. Mrs. Fitzgerald never spoke of her husband again.

A sharp rap on the door brought Sheila back to the cold morning. "Time's God's gift, Sheila, don't waste it." Terry moaned as Sheila slipped out the door and headed down the stairs. Slivers of cold air blew down from the leaky skylight; Sheila was glad the trip to school was only one block.

Mrs. Fitzgerald headed out the door. "There's oatmeal on the stove. Eat it, don't play with it. Put some coal in the furnace, and turn up the heater on the back porch. I want those things dry by the time I get home. Now, I'm cleaning for the McAlesters today, and I'll be home late."

"What about Terry?" Sheila asked, still wiping sleep from her eyes.

"She'll be fine. She can sleep today. God watches out for children," she said as she slid into the cold.

* * * * *

"Verbose. *Verbose.* Don't make me say it again, child of God. And stand up when you answer." Sister Stella Maris loomed over Sheila, not giving her enough room to stand up without backing up at the same time. "Anyone would think *you're* the slow one today!" The class gave a nervous laugh. Sister Stella Maris once told her class she was acknowledged among the other nuns as unusually kind because she never hit a child in anger. Never.

"Verbose," said Sheila. "Wordy." She tucked the pleats of her school uniform against her thin legs and sat down.

Sister's ruler came down hard on the desk, nearly spilling ink from the well. "Never sit down without asking permission," she said, "or until I say you can. Stand up, child, and use your vocabulary word in a sentence. Use a little common sense."

Sheila stood up slowly, still tired from her morning trip to the school to get milk and butter. "*Verbose*. I do not feel at all verbose today."

There was a moment of silence. "Why you *impudent* little—"

The clang of a fire truck right outside the classroom cut off Sister's tirade.

From the front row high-strung Jameson Short shouted above the noise. "Look!" he yelled, "Look! I can see smoke over there!!" He pointed north where whorls of dark smoke hovered above nearby townhouses. As if rehearsed, the entire class ran to the windows. Sheila's view was blocked by her taller classmates.

"Away from those windows! Away!" Sister Stella Maris yanked the hair of some of the boys to make them take their seats. "Let's turn to our elocution lessons, class," she said. "We'll review our vocabulary after lunch."

"Yes, sister," came the chorus of thirty-eight altos.

Sheila thought she could smell smoke.

A few minutes later Mrs. Quinlovan, the office volunteer, opened the classroom door and beckoned Sister to meet with her in the hallway. Sister gave her class instructions to say ten Hail Mary's, and gave them a stern sideways glance—as much as her habit would allow—as she navigated the rows of desks to step out of the classroom. Sister and Mrs. Quinlovan kept their voices low and could not be heard clearly over the murmur of the children. The door opened again, and a crooked finger snaked out of Sister's wide sleeve to beckon Sheila.

"You are to report home immediately," the nun said. "Go now, child. Mrs. Quinlovan will go with you."

Sheila ran down the stairs, nearly tripping as she threw open the old wooden door. Her glasses flew off, and she scrambled to get them. Just as Mrs. Quinlovan caught up with her, Sheila saw her Uncle Pat and Uncle Sean walking toward the school. She ran to them and threw her arms around them both. They smelled like smoke.

"Glory be, child. Hold on. We're here, we just came to get you."

Sheila pulled back, confused. "What's wrong? Sister didn't tell me." Her chin started to quiver. "Ma? Is Ma okay?"

Her uncles looked at each other, then looked at Mrs. Quinlovan. "We'll take care of her, thanks," said Uncle Sean. They each took a hand and walked with her the long block to her street. Parked at a crazy angle across Southwick Street was a dark red fire engine. Sheila saw the Home part of the hopscotch she and Terry drew in the middle of the street last week—last week when Southwick Street was safe and quiet, a large bumpy slate for soft chalk.

Sheila took it all in, piece by piece. The door to Number Eight was open, the beveled glass smashed to smithereens, the lace curtain caught on shards. A fire hose ran from a hydrant on the lower corner of the street—the hydrant they'd passed many times on the way to the beach and never noticed—the hose ran like the evil snake Sister Stella Maris told them about, ran into the house, past imitation Queen Anne furniture brought from Ireland, past the stairs with scratches in the varnish, through the kitchen where Mrs. Fitzgerald's gin stood in a clear bottle on a shelf above an immaculate stove, out to the back porch that was blacker than any sin Sheila ever heard about.

Tattered clothes, smeared with soot, sat and stank in chaotic, wet piles. The walls dripped water, and the painted floor was slippery. The wool coat that just last night was draped across the oil heater—turned over now, its stubby metal legs making it look dead—the coat was stretched across a lump on the unearthed wicker sofa. Just as she saw the fleck of copper at the top of the coat and lunged forward, her Uncle Pat fixed his large hands on Sheila's shoulders and pushed her out the back door. Sheila kicked and cried and tried to reach her sister.

"It's too late, darlin'. It's too late, girl." They led her out the back steps to the alley behind the brownstone. Sheila thought she could hear her mother shrieking in the kitchen.

*   *   *   *   *

Mrs. Fitzgerald never spoke of Terry again. Uncle Sean said the accident was probably caused when the oil heater tipped over, the wool coat catching and fanning out across the laundry; they found a rubber ball under the heater, melted to the floor.

It was a month before Sheila returned to Sister Stella Maris' classroom, a month of silence with her mother, a month of pulling the wagon by herself. On Tuesday it was dairy from St. Ann's, on Thursday it was Commodities for the Needy.

Sister was working with her after school to help her catch up on her vocabulary, but Sheila didn't think Sister would be able to help her find the right words.

Kevin Could Fly

Quebec House Apartment Building, Washington, DC, October, 1962

"Dickie darling, Kevin dear: you young men move back from that television. You'll ruin your eyes, and that wouldn't be too salubrious now, would it?" Scolding us from the big gray chair in the corner of the living room, speaking up over the clink of ice in her highball glass: it was Mother. I heard the *kwhip, kwhip* of her long fingernails sliding across the cushions in search of her cigarette holder. "You young fellows would be better off reading the newspaper or, heaven forefend, reading an improving book."

"Yes, Mom," and "Yes, Mrs. Short." We watched television the way all ten-year-olds watched television—on our tummies, inches away from the set, hands under our chins, knees bent. Kevin and I wiggled back about a foot across the shag carpet, risking major static electric shocks. Our eyes never left the flickering, grainy images of *Superman.*

"I wonder if Superman can drive a car," I said to Kevin.

"Sure, man, I've seen him do it!"

"No lie?" I wanted to believe him.

Mother interceded. "Dickie, one must say *prevaricate*, not lie. Remember, you're never undressed if you have a good vocabulary."

"Do you think Superman can fly backwards?" I was undaunted.

"Sure, man, he can do anything." Kevin D'Arcangelo said it, and that made it so. He seemed so mature and worldly. He was like Superman, I thought, but instead of coming from another planet, he came to DC from Europe. "My dad's the

Principal Deputy Assistant Consul for Political Affairs," he'd told my mother earlier, but that didn't mean much to me. "We moved around all the time." I moved only once, last month from Boston.

But Kevin was better than Superman: there was no Kryptonite in Europe, and he was not hideously susceptible to it anyway. No foreign government or mad scientist could keep Kevin down by waving a clod of dirt in his direction.

"How can he see where he's going when he flies backwards?"

"X-ray vision. Superman can even fly upside-down, man."

Wow! I could never use *man* the way Kevin could. I practiced under my breath. My furtive stage-whispers of Kevin's "no way, *man*" and "hey, *man*" took on a pulse, a rhythm of their own; I tossed my head from side to side, snapping my fingers, throwing my whole dungaree-clad pudgy body into it. In spite of my efforts at secrecy, Mother's radar quivered.

"Just what *is* that susurration?" she asked as I lolled around on the floor. Mother used a voice calculated to make me picture a smile and a small wag of the head. *Nearly perfect,* I thought, *that's almost the way an* Earth woman *would sound.* But I wasn't falling for it, not for a minute.

My so-called mother was really an android from the Planet 77 in Galaxy 88. I spent long afternoons in my room, scribbling down a list of Mother's quirks to prove—most likely while I slept or was in the bathroom—that a switch had been made. Her tearless eyes were my first clue.

The most damning quirk was the shag carpet. The amber-and-orange waves of wool was Mother's—I mean *the android's*—pride and joy. This made sense: Mother, being the product of an alien civilization far in advance of our own, displayed a sense of interior decorating light years ahead of backwater Earth. God, she loved that shag carpet!

"Kevin, you must thank your father for letting you stay overnight with us. I haven't met Principal Deputy Assistant D'Arcangelo *personally*, but I'm sure he's delightful." Mother finished her Campari and tonic; she rose and smoothed her hostess pajamas. "Anyone peckish? Ready for a prandial delight?"

Not waiting for an answer, she asked "Would you lads be dears and run up to Magruder's to fetch another tube of Crest? Our toothpaste just seems to be *evaporating*, but good dentition is a wonderful thing." As Mother spoke, she made small circles with her hands, and pop-bead bracelets orbited her wrists. "Oh, and please fetch some Key Limes. I'd be just *sick with glee* if they had some fresh Key Limes. They sound so *indispensable*."

"Oh, Mom," I protested, "there's this show on about Telstar." An out-of-focus shot of the new satellite flickered on the screen as a scratchy version of the Telstar theme song played. The scene faded; a scientist with a severe crew-cut and white lab coat took off his black-framed glasses to speak directly to us, saying something about space flight.

Mother exercised her adult power by turning off the television. "Go. *With alacrity*. Ride on the sidewalk and don't talk to strangers!" The small dot in the center of the screen faded to black as we raced up the hall and jumped on the elevator to find our bikes.

*   *   *   *   *

Kevin helped me hunt for my rocket-red Schwinn in the dim light of the Quebec House Apartment's basement.

"Man, this place is really creepy," Kevin said. *Yeah,* I thought, *but not as creepy as the roof.* That seven story plunge worried me but still fascinated me.

The time had come to sound out Kevin about Mother. "You know, my mom, well, she's not like other moms," I said. We found our bikes and walked them to the elevator.

"No problem, man. She talks like an English teacher, though."

"She used to be. She's always trying to get me to use big words." I had already absorbed too much of Mother's overstuffed vocabulary; to avoid ridicule from strangers, I pretended I was mute.

"Really? Where'd she teach?"

"Boston." A one word answer, I hoped, would stop more questions.

"Why'd ya leave? Watch the handle bars, man." Kevin held the elevator door as I fumbled with my bike.

"Well." I was embarrassed, and there was so much I didn't understand. But I couldn't lie to my first—and only—friend in my new home. "I'm not real sure. She told me our relatives were embarrassed and wanted us to leave. Something to do with my dad, something about how he died." This was a painful secret, even though I didn't understand exactly what happened. I spent the whole month we'd lived here worried that someone would find out. *When Kevin finds out,* I thought, *he probably won't want to be my friend.*

Jumping on his bike in front of the Quebec House Apartments, Kevin continued with his analysis. "Your mom's kind of religious, isn't she? All those candles, man, don't you worry about a fire?"

"Not really. I think she just likes how they look." How could I explain that the religious candles lining our living room were just another advanced interior-decor touch. Mother found them at Magruder's when she was hunting for marzipan. My favorite was the bright red candle with the picture of the Three Stigmata.

"We all have our quirks," he said over his shoulder as he pedaled hard and pulled a few bike lengths ahead of me.

Yeah! Kevin didn't care!! Kevin was so normal, just as I'd hoped. I stood on my pedals to get more pull and caught up to him in a burst of relief. I'd deliberately picked a friend that was not a freak because I hoped that, one day, when Mother's eccentricities were exposed, people would say, "Yes, but the *boy*, the boy turned out so *normal*. Makes you wonder, doesn't it?"

Kevin would be my cover. Maybe I wouldn't need the birth certificate I'd forged with my new mechanical pencil set, just in case, and left hidden in the copy of *Pilgrim's Progress* Mother gave me for my last birthday.

We pushed on, up and up, up the hill to Magruder's.

*　*　*　*　*

Mother and I usually ate on the couch—we had no table—but tonight she said no, that would not do for company. We brought the large mahogany table with us from Boston—"I love that old leviathan, that *behemoth*," Mother said—but our apartment was just too small and back it went.

Kevin's ingenuity saved the day, or at least dinner. At his suggestion, and under Mother's taut supervision, we closed up her sewing machine and used it as our table. We lit Mother's candles—all twenty-eight of them—and sat down to dinner. "Nothing burnishes a room like candles," Mother said, and laughed at her own joke. Flames winked as the draft from the kitchen window made some of the candles gutter; when the St. Clare's vigil candle blew out, I was told to close the window.

In the steady light, rhinestones from Mother's eyeglasses flashed out small, fake rainbows. My freckles melted in the buttery candle light. Kevin's dark hair glowed with a small aurora borealis. We drew in closer around the sewing machine.

"Thank you, gentlemen, for setting the table. Please pass the sweet potatoes, Dickie." Mother gave Kevin her best hostess smile, and served us. She liked to color-coordinate our meals; we ate from a palette of orange and green, a salute to Autumn. "I hope you enjoy pizza, Kevin."

"Yes, ma'am, mom says I'll eat just about anything. My dad and I ate bugs and squirrels in some of the places we lived, so pizza and sweet potatoes sounds great!" *Did he prevaricate?* I wondered, and hoped he was only exaggerating.

"How nice for you, dear. Do save room for Key Lime cookies." Tiny bands of orange light flew around the room as Mother took a dainty sip of Atomic Tang. "It's my own negus for the Space Age: a heavenly concoction of vodka and a powdered fruit drink," she confided to Kevin.

Mother was warming up to my new friend. She spoke to him as if he were another adult. "I'm very worried about the situation in Cuba, but I have a lot of confidence in President Kennedy. And these days I read so much in the newspaper about another *disagreement* in Europe. Did you see much trouble while you were there?" Mother felt the world's children were always in great peril.

"Sometimes, Mrs. Short. Dad says they usually go after tourists, but when we were overseas we saw someone in our group get dragged away and cut up in the street pretty bad once. That's when Dad said we were coming back. My mom and sister were glad."

"How lugubrious!" Mother was truly alarmed, and eager to change the subject.

"*Lugubrious?*"

"Yes, dear, I think so, too. Dickie, did you remember the toothpaste?"

* * * * *

By the time dinner was over we shared a good mood. We flickered by each other in the galley kitchen, cleaning up and working together as if we had done this before. Kevin washed, I wiped, mother put things away: three notes in a major chord.

"Those green cookies were really delicious, Mrs. Short." Kevin had learned some lessons in diplomacy from his father. I stepped on my foot to keep from laughing.

"Oh, I'm glad you enjoyed them. I thought we could use a little lagniappe. Though the Key Limes weren't quite *chartreuse*, so I practiced a little subterfuge and added a *soupçon* of food coloring," Mother trilled. She made a spiral with her cigarette holder, then gave it quick flick to drop ashes into her cupped hand. Mother did this when she was happy. I thought, *Kevin brings out her shiny side.* "Now, wouldn't a little post-prandial ice cream be ebullient, men?"

"I'm not sure about anything you said except ice cream, and I hope you have vanilla," Kevin said.

"Dickie, will you do the honors? Tonight feels special. I think I'll go get Ethel." Mother gave me an impish look and headed for her bedroom.

Kevin hovered at my elbow in the corner of the kitchen as I struggled to scoop out our frozen dessert. He whispered, "Who's Ethel? Does someone else live here, man?"

Just what—just *how*—could I explain Ethel to Kevin? "Well, she's someone I haven't seen in a couple of years." Before I could elaborate, the record player started blasting scratchy music and we both jumped.

The fluorescent light above our heads flickered on, *crink crink crink.* We turned in unison, and froze against the stove as we stared at the figure in the doorway. Backlit by flickering candles, a tattered orange bathrobe thrown over her clothes—giving bulky flesh to her thin frame—it was Mother! "There's no-o-o business like sho-o-o-w business..."

Her mouth worked wildly, exaggerating the words she sang along with the record. Ethel Merman had come to the Quebec House!

The bathrobe's large chenille sleeves made her arms seem to waddle as she bent her elbows and flailed her arms. Twisting at the waist, my Mother—Mrs. Short, Kevin's hostess, former English teacher—did a slow shimmy to the music. As she vamped and twirled, the fluorescent light caught her thick glasses; she punctuated the lyrics by splaying her fingers and stamping her feet.

The small sound in Kevin's throat became a wild, manic roar. He bent double, grabbing his knees. My laughter left me soundless. To get my breath, I threw myself back against the kitchen wall. Our tears flowed, our noses ran. We shrieked with the abandonment of children. Mother beamed.

Before Miss Merman and Mother could complete their triumph, an irregular thumping penetrated the music. I knew what that meant, and flicked off the record player without lifting the needle. Ethel's brassy soprano voice slid down the scale, taking our high spirits with it.

"What's that?" Kevin asked. We could feel the pounding through our sneakers.

"Oh, it's that *egregious* Elena Muñoz from downstairs," Mother explained to Kevin. "She's been complaining to me at least once a day for the whole month we've lived here. She simply doesn't like us to have a good time." Laying her bathrobe on the big gray chair, Mother confided in Kevin. "She accused me and Dickie of 'dancing the *cha-cha-cha* in stiletto heels.' Of all the temerity!"

"Well, Mrs. Short, my dad tells me 'a good trick is to give them what they don't want'." *What?*

Mother thought a moment. "Kevin, you are wise beyond your years!" She grabbed our hands and glared at the floor. "Take *this*, you corpulent harridan!!" Mother gave her heels a quick click-click-click on the kitchen floor and shook us until we danced along with her. We tittered and stamped like maniacs. Gloom vanished; our good mood was not so fragile after all.

*   *   *   *   *

Kevin and I slurped ice cream and buried ourselves in *Superman* comic books. Mother offered to play Scrabble with us; we passed. She settled down in her favorite chair with a Sloe Gin Fizz to re-read *Mrs. Dalloway.*

"Mom, can we go up to the roof? Tomorrow's Saturday, Mom, no school. And Kevin's never seen it before." I had discovered this special place just last week. Before she could say no, I added, "I think Kevin would really like it." That clinched it.

"Well, for fifteen minutes *only*. Don't forget to extinguish those candles, Dickie. We don't want a conflagration, after all. And mind your acrophobia."

I yelled "Sure, Mom," over my shoulder; we were already half way out the door.

*   *   *   *   *

The broad, flat roof of the Quebec House was a sea of small brown stones; a boardwalk of weathered gray planks marked where it was safe to walk. Large wooden deck chairs faced south for sunbathing. Rock Creek Park flowed behind the building, an ocean of trees moving under an ocean of air; dark green waves crested up from the soft darkness. Leaves sighed and lapped against hard wood, foaming in the security lights. The roof floated above this sea.

In the failing light, our side street was a dark stream flowing into the Connecticut Avenue river; amber street lights marked its distant, glowing shore.

As Kevin and I burst out from the elevator—our bathysphere—the full moon was born.

"Man oh man oh man!" Kevin spun around and around; I could hear the stones crunch under his sneakers as he left the safety of the wooden walkway. "What's that, that thing that looks like a space ship over there?" He pointed to a church tower jutting up through distant trees, outlined in blinking red lights.

"The National Cathedral. Right over there, with those neon lights, that's the Uptown Theatre. The zoo's down that way about half a mile. Sometimes you can hear the gibbons howl like a crazy alarm clock." I followed behind Kevin as he inspected the perimeter of the rooftop; he kicked a few stones over the edge. The roof didn't seem so creepy with Kevin here, but my stomach and brain began to reel from the seven-story drop. The safety of our second floor apartment seemed so distant. "Maybe we should sit down." We flopped onto the wooden chairs.

"This is *great*. If I lived here, I'd *never* come down, man. I'd eat up here, and even *sleep* up here! I love being up high."

"I'll bet you've been on plenty of airplane trips. Right?"

"Yeah, sure, but this is better!"

We were quiet for a few minutes. Overhead, Telstar swam among the stars. In the silence I heard, "Hey, Dickie?"

"Please don't call me that!! Call me Richie."

Kevin laughed. "Yeah, man, you must get kidded about your name *a lot*!" I didn't need to be reminded. The kindest taunt was *Dickie, Dickie, Dick-tionary*. "What happened to your father, man?"

"He died last year. Some kind of car accident. His car went off a bridge. There was something about an inquest, I didn't really understand it. I had to go to see this lady counselor for a while after that."

"How come?"

"Well," I said, "Mom said it was because I didn't cry after Pop died, so she sent me there. But I tried to explain to the lady that Mom didn't cry, so I shouldn't." I pushed my sneaker through the boards and poked at some stones. "It was kind of weird. The lady was real upset all the time. She ate all the time I was talking, and told me she didn't understand me."

There were so many things I didn't understand, like that morning last year, that morning in Boston. I'd come back from the bus stop to pick up my forgotten homework. No one heard me come in; I was halfway up the stairs when I heard adult voices in the kitchen; the tone in my uncle's voice made me stop. He was speaking to Mother.

I could see Uncle Ralph in my mind as he spoke, I could see his ugly mouth, jammed with too many teeth. "It's just not normal, Sheila. The boy's *peculiar* if you ask me. A boy should grieve for his father. Maybe he's *ashamed*." He snapped his newspaper for emphasis; I was sure he would hide behind it. "He needs help. *You* might talk to that doctor, too. Frankly, our whole family is embarrassed. You know what people are saying."

With a soft, steel voice I'd heard her start to use lately, Mother said, "Ralph Short, shame on *you*. Jameson was your brother!"

"He was weak. Couldn't cut it." The clink of a coffee cup on a saucer.

"And you know Dickie's introverted. And precocious, at least intellectually." She paused, and said in a drier voice, "But you are correct, he has not been visibly morose—not enough to satisfy *some* people. I'll make an appointment for him with that counselor. But after the inquest, if the insurance company won't pay, we'll leave."

"Fine." He sniffed, then added, "He's not really *hurt*, it's just his feelings."

Throat lumps choked me.

The early October breeze turned cool. Kevin and I were quiet as the elevator sank down to the second floor.

* * * * *

"Time for bed, young sirs, even if it is Friday. Ravel up that knitted sleeve. I'm going to my room to read. Don't forget to brush."

"Night, Mom," and "Good night, Mrs. Short."

"Don't stay up too late. I'll make a special breakfast tomorrow morning. 'Having something to look forward to is a form of wealth,' my Aunt Marge always says." While we completed our dental assignment, I could hear Mother humming her alter ego's theme song as she went about her nightly ritual: first she placed a chair under the front doorknob, then she opened the kitchen window wide to "expunge" the cigarette smoke.

"Flip ya for the top bunk, man," Kevin offered. "But I can sleep anywhere, any time."

"Wish I could. But nah, that's okay. I like to sleep on the bottom bed." Acrophobia. Even living on the second floor made me nervous.

We changed into our tee shirts and shorts, turned out the light, and hopped into the bunk beds by the green glow of the night light. I heard Mother's bedroom door close.

I stuck my foot into the mattress above my head. "Kevin, you asleep?"

"Not yet, man."

"Do you think Superman is really dead?" I cried for many nights after George Reeve's suicide. That was three years ago, and I still couldn't accept it.

"Just the *actor*, man, just the actor. But that's not real life, Richie. Don't get them mixed up. Reeve's let us down, man, he was really stupid."

But we could bring Superman back to life, right there, right then. We could play Superman and have secret identities. Kevin found a problem when I told him my plan.

"*You* can't be Superman, Richie, Superman doesn't have freckles. People would know who you really are."

"I can fix that. Hold on, I'll be right back." By the time Kevin climbed down from the top bunk I was back from my dash across the hall to the bathroom. I handed Kevin the pair of Mother's reading glasses she kept on shelf by the shower. "Here. Put these on, *Clark*." Perfect.

"What are you *doing,* man?" Kevin stood beside me, blinking wildly in the mirror as he tried to focus through Mother's thick cats-eye glasses. He watched my dim green reflection as I tied a towel around my neck to look like a cape, then tucked it in the back of my tee shirt. I almost finished hiding my freckles with layers of toothpaste when we heard a soft knock at the door. *Uh-oh.*

"Dickie. Kevin. It is I. Do I hear voices?" Mother swung the door open. She looked at us in the Krypton-green light, first at me, then at Kevin. There we stood: one man split into his two identities, doubled back through the mirror.

"Words fail me," she said faintly, and closed the door. A moment later I heard her sigh and, in a voice more like Mother's, said: "Please clean up and go to sleep."

*   *   *   *   *

I was nearly asleep when Kevin said, "Richie, you awake, man?"

"Mmmm."

"I shoulda been Superman. I'm the one that can fly."

"Okay, maybe next time," I burbled. "But no more toothpaste, okay?"

"No, I really mean it." Sleep was pulling me down, I only half heard him. He leaned over the edge of the top bunk. "Let's set the alarm for midnight. No: *three o'clock.* Then we can go up on the roof. I'll show you. You can fly, too, man. It's all the way you cup your hands. That's the secret." He waved his hands like a crab.

Only the lower portion of my brain was awake. Like a robot or someone hypnotized in a grade B movie, I set the alarm then drifted down. Giant space apes, screaming as they plunged off bridges, haunted my sleep.

*   *   *   *   *

"Dickie, darling, Kevin, dear: *Rise and shine*, soldiers! It's almost nine o'clock." A sing-song voice came through the bedroom door; it was Mother. She knocked once, then entered. Crisp morning air flowed into the room from the kitchen window, along with some strange food odors. "Come and get some fresh Key Lime muffins while they're hot, and some nice chocolate pancakes." I groaned: *green and brown food for breakfast!* I pulled the covers over my head for warmth, waiting for Mother to pull them down, to throw me into the day.

But I didn't hear anything.

Mother's voice was a little husky when she asked in a slow, deliberate voice, "Dickie, where is Kevin?"

"Top bunk."

"*Dickie.*" There was command in her voice, and I jumped out of bed. I picked up my Baby Ben; it said four fifteen. The alarm was turned off. *Did I dream everything last night?*

Mother was standing rigid in the middle of the room, looking at the empty top bunk. She shook me by the shoulders—the first time I could remember my mother touching me in years—as her voice rose to a shrill crescendo. "Dickie. Where. IS. *KEVIN!*"

Her eyes followed mine to the bathroom. But no, I could see it was empty from where I stood.

"Oh, sweet Jesus! That poor boy!!" Mother pivoted toward the open door. Her legs made long scissors, cutting across the bedroom, past the bathroom, and into the living room. I trailed her. She stopped at the front door and stared: the chair under the knob was pushed aside.

Then small muscles began to move in her face. I could almost hear—almost *see*—what she was thinking, each thought snapping together like pop-beads in her bracelet:

All children are in danger all the time. *Pop!*

The kitchen window is open. *Pop!*

The chair is gone from the doorknob. *Pop!*

Kevin's father is almost a diplomat. *Pop!*

Kevin is missing. *Pop!*

Kevin has been kidnapped!!!

"Check the hallways, ask the neighbors, check with the front desk," she ordered, back in control. "I'll telephone Mrs. D'Arcangelo." She sank into her chair, her eyes half closed. With her address book open in her lap, her fingernail poised to dial, she put down the receiver.

"Dickie." She stood up and looked at me with wide, clear eyes. Thin arms encircled me. As she pressed me close and leaned her chin on my head, I could smell cigarette smoke and her breakfast beer. Then the android—I mean *my mother*—cried. I cried, too, as I thought about Mother and George Reeves and Superman. And my father.

She whispered, "Find him. We *need* him. I need you—."

A soft knock on the front door stopped us both. We waited, unsure if we heard the knock, unsure what to do about anything. Another knock, and we started for the door together.

Even before the door opened, *I knew*. The hallways would be empty, the neighbors would not know anything. But everything would be fine now—*he didn't leave us*. I knew my name was Richie, I was Superman with freckles, and that my mother loved me. With my cheeks tight from dried tears, I cupped my hands to show Kevin that now *I* knew the secret to flying, *man*, now I knew.

Gertrude

Broken Bone, Colorado,
Easter Sunday, 1998

Boulder was a picture postcard in the rearview mirror. The road ahead seemed unnaturally straight. Eyes forward, mind sky-clear, hands in the ten-and-two position: it was an easy drive for our little truck, but I wanted to talk to my new friend Sandro before we got to Broken Bone.

"I've never brought anyone to Easter before, not to the family home," I said. "Not to *my* family." As I thought of my brother, his wife, her daughter, as all-American as lemon custard pie, I felt my mouth twist.

"Never? What about all those *others*?" Sandro gave me a buddy punch. I'd known him a month, and dared myself to ask him along. Turning forty last month made me more cautious and more reckless.

"Yeah. Sure." The wind rushed down from the mountains and toyed with the truck. The heater was colder than outside, and I could feel the icy seat through my jeans. I turned the back wipers on and off to clear the late morning frost, then checked to make sure the high beams weren't on. "Sure wish Easter was later this year. No leaves on the trees yet."

"Marshall O'Malley, why are you so fidgety? Something you're not telling me?"

"Just that Broken Bone's not like DC, that Super Sodom you come from." I'd never been to DC, but about twenty years ago I left Broken Bone and moved to Boulder for college and stayed there, making my way back to my brother's house for Family Days of Obligation. Boulder changed my life. It was close to Broken Bone, but just not the same.

"Oh, I don't know. I like it here," Sandro said, as he inspected the contents of the glove box. "Nice flares, Marsh. You look ready for almost anything. And it's nearly a new century; anything can happen." He turned to look at me, and said emphatically, "It's small consolation, but it usually doesn't."

We rode in silence for a few miles, alone on the road. Caramel ground traveled along beside us. An apple pie sat between us, smelling sweet and tart, my traditional contribution to all family meals. I snapped on the radio, always tuned to KWYR. Céline Dion covered up the wind and the noise of the tires on US 25. I could see the top of the Rockies in the mirror, jagged like cloth cut with pinking shears.

"When I was a kid," I said over the radio's song of love gone wrong, "my brother told me the mountains used to cover the sky, then God cut them in half so people could see the stars."

"You're making that up," Sandro said, and drew a tic-tac-toe in the window frost.

"Yup." I took my hand from the two position and punched his massive arm, but kept my eyes in motion, moving from the mirror to dashboard every five seconds, just the way I'd seen in safety films.

"Never kid a kidder," he said, and exhaled hot breath on the window to fog the puzzle.

"That's what I've heard. Why not?"

Sandro leaned over the back of the seat, checking out the storage compartment. "You don't want to know." He twisted back around and said, "My God, Marshall, what's with all the emergency equipment back there? Are you *expecting* a disaster? You're sure a *worrier*, aren't you?"

"Well, I don't *feel* prepared. I mean, an axle could break or we could hit a hidden rock."

Sandro returned to his puzzle. Sometimes I thought the truck's engine was saying words I couldn't quite understand. "Wait a minute, Marshall. And I don't mean stop the truck. I mean, what in thunder is that over there?" Sandro reached across my chest and pointed west to the dark clouds in the sky. "Looks like rain, but—?"

"That's *virga*. A special rain. It's so dry here, the rain never makes it all the way down. Sometimes a storm never happens. Father Nature at his strangest!"

"That's certainly different. Not at all what I would expect. But you're not kidding a kidder, are you?"

He laughed a full, deep laugh; before I could get defensive I started to laugh, too.

"Oh, about my brother," I said, "Please don't freak out. We look a *lot* alike. Same voice, same habits. Jake does a good impression of me." Jake was more like a father and mother to me since our folks died in a car crash; I was still a kid, Jake was just starting out.

"Just how *much* alike are you?"

"Not *that* much alike," I said, and picked up speed.

"Relax, Marsh," Sandro said and squeezed my shoulder. "I can tell you're worried."

I tapped the oil light; no obvious signs of danger there. "Don't *you* ever worry?"

"Nah," he said, "I don't worry, I'm *Italian!* Third generation, but genes are genes. It's just our nature, a D'Arcangelo family trait. Besides, just how strange can *your* family be?"

Oh, God!! This could be a real goat rope.

"Look. We're almost there." I pointed to a road sign with a prairie dog nearly invisible in its cold shadow. "That little town we just went through was Close Shave. Only a few more minutes. Jake would say we'll have to 'grease a fat hog' to get there in time for dinner."

Sandro smiled. I thought the heater was warming up. "Oh," I added quietly, "Don't worry about Dotty. She's just visiting."

"Who? What do you mean—"

"We're here!" Gravel crunched as we pulled into the driveway. I honked the horn and killed the engine. "Welcome to Toad Hall. Grab the pie and let's go. We're nearly late!"

*   *   *   *   *

The clock struck two as we walked into the overheated family room. Bucky, an aging border collie, barked our arrival and ran around our feet, but didn't dare follow us into the rest of the house. Last year Jake and Bucky spent a week at obedience school, and lessons were learned.

The family was already seated around the enormous dining room table my mother bought just before she died. *I remember our first meal at the table, how Mom looked at me and Jake and Dad, and said she wanted to see lots of grandchildren eating with us, that our new table gave us plenty of room. What would she think of us now, each person was an island, pulled back into ourselves?*

At the head of the table was Jake. Tall, ruddy and still freckled, he seemed to take up the chair and most of the table.

As we walked in, Jake stood, said howdy, shook Sandro's hand, and sat again. "Marsh," he said as he carved the ham, "give your friend a seat." He waved to the empty chairs.

"Oh, good, just in time, we just sat down," my sister-in-law trilled. Lydia half rose from her chair and gave me a hug. "Why, Marsh, this must be your friend. Have a seat, hon. We're just saying grace. And may God not strike any heathens dead for hypocrisy." She gave my brother a pointed look.

Lydia once told me she was trying to civilize my brother. Her crusade was doomed, but she was not about to give up even though she went to Easter service alone that morning. "Sometimes all it takes is the right person to set you straight," she'd said.

Lydia smiled at Sandro. "Mr. D'Arcangelo, this is my daughter Aria." My niece bent her head down, but kept her eyes glued on Sandro. Twelve is an awful age. She started to speak, but a sharp look from Jake cut her off.

Lydia's mother, Dotty, sat beside Sandro and started a conversation about the mashed potatoes. "My, aren't these nice," she said, not quite looking at him. "Didn't have potatoes like this when I was a girl, no sir. And there's so many to choose from! New kinds of potatoes nearly every year it seems to me. Like the time we were camping, and Lydie's uncle, a real city boy, used poison ivy for loo paper. Lydie, how about some more of that nice bourbon, please. We had some nice bourbon once at Christmas. I like to make those black-bottom cupcakes at Christmas." Lydia chalks up a lot to her mother's stroke, but I've never been sure.

When dinner started, we were polite and quiet except for Dotty's continuous talking. That's her tradition. Halfway through the meal, Lydia jumped up to get the biscuits she almost forgot; that's *her* tradition. Jake tossed one to me, and I caught it without looking, as if I expected it. Dotty's chatter drove him crazy, and I could picture Jake picturing me stuffing the biscuit real hard into Dotty's mouth— probably when she stopped for a bit just to wheeze in and out but not to stop completely. Our side of the family isn't too much for talking.

But I did warn Sandro not to get Jake going about how Nixon was right. "Don't bring up politics," I'd told Sandro, "Jake looks like me but thinks like Archie Bunker." About twenty years back, during one of the first Family Days of

Obligation I tried to change the subject when Jake started in about Watergate. I'd just moved to Boulder and felt more Jake's equal. So I finally said, "That Jake, you just can't get an opinion out of him." A few moments of silence, then more about how Nixon was framed. He was close to me, but just not the same.

My niece was flirting with Sandro, a fork in one hand and the other busy twisting her hair. "How long have you lived in Boulder, Mr. D'Arcangelo?" Aria giggled and looked down, the top of her blonde head shining across the table to Sandro.

"Please," he said smoothly, "call me Sandro." She looked up as he winked; she giggled again and flashed a smile full of braces at his dark good looks. "I moved here a few months ago, last fall, straight—*fresh*—from DC. I'm a real city boy. Glad I did."

"Wow," she said, "your eyes are so brown I can't see those dark things in the middle."

Lydia leaned toward her and said quietly, "They're *pupils*, dear. And it's not polite to say personal things, remember?"

Sandro laughed. "It's okay. Just because you can't see something, doesn't mean it isn't there!" He winked one eye and then the other, and Aria winked back.

But Dotty jumped in before my niece could flirt again. "Well, you won't catch me going to Washington. I can tell you *Boulder's* bad enough, all those weird people there. Marshall, how can you *stand* Boulder? I remember going there once and saw a *man* walking down the street in a Girl Scout uniform! My stars, can you imagine? Just like one of Lydia's troop. I mean, why would a *grown man* want to—"

"Don't the mashed potatoes look like Walter Matthau?" I asked the entire group and held the dish up for inspection.

In the momentary silence, I could hear Dotty thumping her legs against the chair. She kept them in motion when she talked, and sometimes forgot to stop them when her mouth closed.

"Sandro, Marshall told me you're a professor. What do you teach?" Jake asked. He looked at Sandro with my face.

"Political Science," he lied, and I kicked him under the table. Hard. We both taught Computer Science. He once told me that Computer Science is the hairdressing of the 90's. "And no, I think the potatoes look like Bill Clinton. Tell me, Jake, don't you think the press is awful tough on him? Bill Clinton, I mean?"

Lydia jumped up to get more bourbon. I think she knew what was coming. I know I did. There was nothing in my truck that could help me now.

I turned to Dotty and asked, "How's tricks?" It was like turning on the radio to drown out TV. I couldn't hear Jake and Sandro too well over Dotty's babble and thumping and Bucky barking from the family room, but there were strange, choking sorts of noises coming from my brother. A real goat rope.

"Well, all I can say is they get the best jobs at the plant," I heard Jake say when Dotty stopped long enough to help herself to a fresh glass of bourbon. Jake looked flushed. "But I wouldn't want my sister to marry one!"

Then Lydia—making little brooms with her bent wrists—swept us out of our chairs. "I need to clear the table, and who wants pie, and go sit in the family room." Jake got up from his place at the head of the table. His red face clashed with his auburn hair.

But Jake had Sandro's shoulder in a firm grip, and Jake was *laughing!*

You can relax now, Marsh, just like everyone keeps telling you. No broken axles on this trip!

*   *   *   *   *

I looked hard at the TV, always worried I'd see something I shouldn't, some secret thing accidentally on the air. Beside me, Dotty's thin legs hung over the edge of the plaid couch. Right, left, right, left: she swung her legs against the front of our seats, keeping time to the beat inside her head. She said—well, she said just about everything, and didn't stop for periods or paragraphs, and kept saying everything as we sat and digested our dinner. The Easter decorations in the neighborhood weren't especially good this year, she told us, but then all of Broken Bone, maybe even all of Colorado, was slipping just a little in that department.

Lydia got dessert ready so we could have it when we got back from our walk. Aria was pulling at Sandro's belt loops. Jake fiddled with the big lever on his recliner and navigated the TV remote. Bucky barked and jumped, then nuzzled Sandro's jeans where the seams don't show.

I stretched, yawned loudly, and stood up, right in front of the TV that held the family captive. "Ready for our walk?" I'd started a Family Walk to break up the Days of Obligation a few years back; that's *my* tradition. Just a quick once-around Lake No One, the dried-up pond at the end of the block. Bucky barked and everyone groaned as we reached for our coats.

"Oh, no. I can't go," Dotty said. She sat down.

"Why not, Mom? The doctor said walking is good for you." Lydia's voice was concern and frustration. "You don't want another stroke, do you?"

Dotty looked around the room and said, "We're an odd lot." Bucky stopped barking.

"What do you mean?" Sandro asked.

"*What?* Oh. I get it." Lydia pointed around the room and counted. "No we're not, Mom. See? There's six of us this year. That's an *even* number."

Dotty stood up and reached for my elbow.

"What do you mean, Dotty?" Sandro asked again. He stopped in front of us—Aria pulling at his scarf—and looked directly at Dotty. His brown eyes found faded china blue behind her watery glasses.

"Well, when I was a girl we used to go for walks after parties, but we had to go in pairs. One time I was at a party and there was a boy I didn't know and I wanted to walk with him but my girlfriends pulled me away and said no."

"Why was that?"

"They called him *Gertrude*. You know, a real girly boy. I didn't know."

"So what did you do?"

"I didn't go." She shrugged her thin shoulders.

"Well," said Sandro, "times have changed, haven't they?"

"Oh, yes," Dotty started, "why I can remember—"

His eyes sparkled. "Walk with me. Walk with *us*." I think I saw Dotty blush as she took his arm; he and I escorted her out the door.

*   *   *   *   *

Broken Bone's twisted cottonwoods—decorated with Easter eggs on strings—shrunk to the size of party favors in the rearview mirror, and the road home spread out before us. KWYR was treating us to more Céline Dion. I snapped off the radio so we could hear the big music.

"Just *what* did you say to Jake?"

"Oh, nothing much." Sandro was breathing hot air on the window, and drawing a heart.

"Come on, never kid a kidder, remember?"

"I just told him about being Italian."

I gave him my special sidelong look of disbelief, just the way I'd seen Jake do a thousand times. "Seriously."

"Don't you remember? I told you. Jake was starting in about—well, *different ethnic groups*, to put it politely—and I told him that we Italian men don't consider ourselves white. At least not in the D'Arcangelo family. He took it as a joke."

Before that sunk in, Sandro leaned toward me—right across where the pie had been—and reached across my chest. He pointed out the window with a beefy finger, due west. "Look at that! *Virga*, right? See, sometimes we know things if we see them enough times."

Miles away—toward Utah—dirty clouds dropped rain lines almost to the ground.

On the road home we talked and laughed and didn't even notice the stars through the top of the sky.

Marked Man

Skydown Towers Apartments, St. Petersburg, Florida
Independence Day, 1998

"Now, Tripper, what would make a good murder weapon?" Victoria stood in the middle of her tiny kitchen and spoke to the small dog at her feet, wagging its tail as she spoke. "By *good*, of course, I mean one that wouldn't get me convicted!" Tripper stopped wagging his stubby tail when Victoria stopped moving her lips.

She bent down and held the Cocker's jet black head in her hands.

"Poor Tripper. You're getting about deaf as a post, aren't you sweetie? Guess we all go downhill one way or th'other. It's nothin' we *plan*. Good and bad things just happen, right pups? Otherwise you'd point right at something, something that won't hold fingerprints, right sweetie?"

He pulled away and shook his head like a propeller flying against the tickle in his ears. His leash jangled, the metal clasp hitting the floor. "Poor baby," she cooed again, "it's a sin and a shame he makes you wear that noose in the house. I'm sure you won't try to run away again, will you hon? He just didn't have to be so mean! Bad enough he made you too afraid to bark. That was just cruel, baby."

The dog licked her face, then got busy sniffing the tiled floor.

Victoria leaned over the sink and squinted out the window; there, on the minute balcony in the bright Florida sun, she saw the back of a shaved head stuck up over the top of a lawn chair. *Hunh. Him!! That melon head of his. Reckon it's the only part of him that isn't tattooed. Cartoon fool!!*

Kneeling down in front of the sink, she opened the cabinet, crawled most of the way in and continued talking to her near-deaf dog. "Let's see what we got here. Drano? Nah, too trite. Mr. Clean just isn't strong enough. And I'm certainly not wasting my good Lestoil. Bet a nice fels naptha salad would do the trick, if only that slob ate salad."

The small dog rubbed his nose against Victoria's bare leg; her miniskirt rode higher as she wiggled around. "Tripper, aren't you just the least bit *tired* of his liquids and *gasses?*" she asked, her voice muffled in the arsenal of household cleaners. Tripper nibbled at her painted toes and Victoria giggled involuntarily.

No, I guess you don't mind, little doggie. You're so eager to please, you probably wouldn't mind if he pulled your tail. But I sure mind. Damn him! And damn all that legal crap keepin' my money hostage.. Alls I know is if I leave him I lose it all!

She backed out of the cabinet, adjusted her skirt down and stood up—too fast. The quick motion, and years of menthol cigarettes, made her woozy. *Lordie, I'm getting too old for this!* She looked around the cramped kitchen for a lethal device as she propped herself against the fridge. Then she saw it on top of the cabinets: the perfect weapon! The chrome toaster her sister gave her as a wedding present thirty years ago, the one he said was a piece of junk, the one he refused to use—it was just the ticket. *And it would be so easy to clean.* Then she sighed.

"Nope," she said, and bent to pick up Tripper, "nope, I'm not gonna do it with that thing. That's about the last new thing we ever had in this place. Kinda sad it's never been used. We'll never know how good it could be!" Tripper licked her ear then jumped down, making a small circle several times that wound his leash around her legs.

"Silly boy," she said as she unfurled his leash. He went back to scratching his ears.

Fishing with her toes, she grabbed the slippers she kept under the kitchenette table, tossed her tightly-permed, carefully-dyed head at the dog and said, "Come on, hush puppy, let's check out the bathroom." She pointed the way.

Walking behind the zig-zagging dog, she stepped nimbly to avoid the dance of his leash.

*　*　*　*　*

Skydown Towers stood higher than its neighbors on Central Avenue, an aging beacon for retirees and Section 8 tenants throughout St. Petersburg. Small balconies stuck out from the unadorned building, a last-minute change in the architect's plan. The balcony on the top floor suffered the mid-day sun without the protection of an upper floor neighbor. The tiny slab of concrete was just big enough to hold a sagging aluminum lawn chair and its massive occupant.

"Bugger you! Don't tell me you can't ink me today. After all the business I've given you. Bugger you good. Damn damn damn." Neal jammed the antenna back into the phone, and tried to slam the soft disconnect button. His hands, gnarled from too many years running a wrecking ball, didn't give him much control. "Damn it to hell," he barked, and rammed the cordless phone into the back pocket of his sagging shorts.

He reached into the front pocket of his shorts and carefully laid out its contents on the dented railing: a cigar cutter, a lighter, a big cheap cigar, and a bottle of moisturizer. Methodically he cut the stogie, then sent the tip on a long arc over the railing. He lit the cigar and took a deep drag; small, dead ashes dropped to the worn green indoor-outdoor carpet. A few live cinders smoldered, making new holes among the old. Neal showed his satisfaction by breaking wind for several long seconds.

"I'll just drive out to the freakin' beach tonight and find a tourist place that's open. Someone's gotta be open," he said, adding another wind-breaking moment as punctuation. "Damn tootin'," he said, half-smiling at his own joke.

Then he frowned. "Just how the holy hell can I get a tattoo when they keep closin' for holidays? And what's so damn special about the Fourth of July I'd just like to know." He glared at the flag that Victoria had taped to the railing, and gave it a gassy salute.

Using a jagged fingernail, Neal traced the one blank spot on his left forearm. The small white outline melted into his flesh that was turning a deeper mottled, rare-steak pink in the sun. "Right *there*, that's where I want the next one. Where'd I put that picture?" He grabbed the shaky railing to pull himself half out of the chair, nearly tipping it over. Groaning, he pulled a folded piece of paper from the back pocket of his shorts. Falling back into the chair, he smoothed the creased paper against the hemisphere of his stomach.

"Right *there*, that's where I want the next one," he repeated, and wrapped the photocopy of a small beagle around the blank spot on his arm. "My Chico," he half-whispered, his voice thick with cigar phlegm. "God took you, but I'm gonna keep you. So what if it doesn't look exactly like you. What goes the way we plan?" He ended the philosophy and solemn promise to the dead dog's image with a sincere belch.

For the next few minutes he rubbed moisturizer on his arms and legs to preserve the inked renderings of his previous pets. "Damn killer sun," he griped, and glared upward at the intense noon sky. "Sure as hell wish it'd rain."

His reverie was broken by a screech from the bathroom window right next to the balcony.

"Neal Welden, you get out of that damn sun before you have another sunstroke. This time you can be damned sure I just won't be bothered to take you to the ER." Victoria pushed as much of her small head as she could through the rippled jalousie window to make sure he could hear her yell.

He shrugged, and ground his cigar into the pitted fake grass with his sandal.

"And another thing," Victoria bellowed, "where the *sam fat* is the damn boric acid?" She pulled herself back in the window, then seconds later emerged again and added in a softer tone, "I need it for roaches."

"We *got* roaches," he snarled.

"To get *rid of 'em*, I mean."

"Don't know. Now close the freakin' window before you let all the cold air out."

Without stopping to think, Victoria cranked the window closed, hard enough to crunch the glass panes in the metal frame.

Neal rubbed himself with more moisturizer and watched a limp breeze play with the flag.

*   *   *   *   *

"Damn his eyes. He even makes it hard to kill him!" Victoria sat down on the pink chenille toilet seat cover with as much of a thump as her small body could make. Momentarily giving up on her search for a weapon, she fished a crumpled cigarette out of the pocket in her blouse. Lighting up and dragging deeply, she leaned back against the cool porcelain toilet tank. The porcelain tank cover scraped as it slid backwards. "Tripper, now cut that out." She pulled the Cocker away from the bathtub where he was slurping water from her second morning shower. Balancing her cigarette on the crocheted toilet-paper holder, she coiled the dog's leash around her wrist, then picked him up. He jumped down and began sniffing the bathroom floor tiles.

Yanking open the medicine cabinet mirror, she did a quick inventory of its contents but found nothing lethal. She slammed the cabinet shut and leaned close to study her face. "You're lucky, Tripper, you don't need to worry about bags under your eyes," she said as she pulled her freckled skin taut beside her pale gray eyes. "Not pretty as pink, but not bad for mid-fifties either. That gravity'll get ya every time. Sure am looking longer in the tooth than I'd like." She sat down again and took another drag.

"You know, I wouldn't *have* to hunt for a murderous instrument if he'd just *behave*. Alls I ask is for a little respect, right doggy? Just some common courtesy, for cryin' out loud. And someone with a nicer temper, too, if I get to wish. Lordie, that man can rage!!" She took another deep drag, then picked up Tripper and cradled him like a baby.

"Now, I don't need to tell *you*, of all people, that some men cheat and some men lie like *dogs*. No offense. But why'd *I* have to get one that—" She was cut short by the bang of the balcony door sliding closed. "Damn. Hop down, sweetie. He's back." She flushed her cigarette.

Holding Tripper's leash tightly, she shooed the dog into the hallway; they squeezed past Neal on his march into the bathroom.

"How about closing the door this time?" she yelled over her shoulder. The only response she got was bathroom noises. "Guess it's asking too much to wash his hands," she muttered. Settling into the oversized naugahyde recliner, as far away from the bathroom as she could get in the tiny living room, she reached for the remote. The dog scrambled in beside her and nestled under her arm.

Victoria was nearly asleep when Neal threw himself on the couch.

Looking at a battered black-and-white television he barked, "What is this crap? Where's the damned remote?" He saw it in Victoria's lap and snapped, "Toss it here." The remote made a long, slow arc as she tossed it to him. He aimed it at the television.

"Neal, *wait!* This is *Hitchcock*, fer pity's sake. You know, the movie with Kim what's-her-name. The one you like, with the big eyebrows."

"Kovak. Kim *Kovak*," he grunted, and scratched his sunburned neck.

"Okay, could even been Novak for all I care" she said, noncommittally, and rubbed the dog's belly.

"Just push him down the stairs," Neal coached the movie, "then jump yourself." They watched the small tube as the actress fell to her death.

Neal got up and went into the bedroom. "Anyone calls, I'm not home," he said as he flopped onto the bed. The springs protested their load.

A few moments later Neal's loud snores became regular. Victoria got up and closed the bedroom door. She picked up the Princess phone from the cluttered table beside the couch and took it out to the balcony. She slid the door nearly closed, taking care not to sever the extra-long cord. Sitting cross-legged on the scrappy green carpet with her back to the sky she said aloud, "Lordie, why couldn't we live on the first floor? One day I'm gonna lose my lunch just lookin' over the edge this high up."

Inside, she could see Tripper pressing his nose against the thin crack in the sliding glass door, and hear the throaty whisper he used for a bark. "Hush, hon," she said, "I'll be right back in. Just settle down, poochie."

She cradled the turquoise receiver under her chin and used her pink fingernails to dial, the night-light glow of the buttons obscured by the sun. The receiver purred softly in her ear.

"Good afternoon. Mrs. Lobosco speaking." The cultured soprano voice, with its Boston accent, was a sharp contrast to Victoria's flat Western speech.

"Celeste, it's me, honey! Hope I didn't get you outta the shower."

"Why hello, Victoria! No, my dear, I've been dry for *hours*. Would you enjoy coming down for some nice cold duck and lasagna? We were planning to have frankfurters for the holiday, but Joseph said no, my dear, don't forget that we are also Italian! He would still adore some baked beans, though. He's just *salivating* for some of your lasagna. When can you pop in?" Celeste didn't give Victoria a chance to interrupt until she stopped to breathe.

"Celeste. *Celeste!* Hold on, hon. I *can't* come down right now."

The other end of the line was momentarily quiet. "Why ever not, Victoria? Joseph is so looking forward to some of your delicious lasagna. I was rather hoping we could have a play date for your little Tripper and our little Betsy. They make such a marvelous couple, don't they? Tripper's gorgeous Cocker looks, and Betsy's adorable Sheltie heritage. Really, I was telling Mrs. Walker down on four, just the other day, that they really ought—"

"No. No, it's not that. There's no lasagna."

"What?" Another momentary pause. "Why, just this morning I was getting Joseph's breakfast and I could detect that wonderful aroma all the way down here on five. We were positively drooling. I could detect it again when I took Betsy for her morning constitutional. No lasagna? My dear, was that an olfactory illusion?"

Victoria was silent. She could picture the thin face of her friend, pinched with concern.

"Victoria. What is going on?"

"There's no lasagna. Well, I mean, there *was*, and now there isn't." *Wish I had my Kools. And sure as all get-out wish I was back in Broken Bone! Oh, sweet Colorado.*

"Tosh and tutty-kins! Don't be ludicrous, Victoria. I've known you for years. We're like each others' diaries. Just speak frankly, my dear, and remember to breathe!"

"I baked it up this morning and stuck it in the fridge. Neal came home from his poker game and ate some." She wiped the sweat from the back of her neck and hoped she wasn't getting too much sun. She glanced over her shoulder. *Is that a cloud?* "But he left it out. For hours."

She could hear the anger rising in her voice as she spoke. She cleared her throat. "He left the whole damn thing out to go bad. Nearly drove Tripper crazy. I came back from Publix and the whole place just reeked. You know it's like an oven in here." *If that* tightwad *would just let me run the AC a little more it wouldn't be so bad. You'd think it was* his *money we were spendin'. Shoulda put the damned lasagna back in the fridge and let those bacteria finish him off.*

"You poor dear! I'm so sorry. All that hard work, and—"

"Oh, it's not just that. Really."

"My dear, I'm sure whatever problems you are having can be managed quite nicely. Whenever Joseph and I are quarrelsome, we usually sit down and have a nice—"

"We haven't had sex in twelve years," Victoria blurted out.

Another silence, longer than the others.

"Twelve. *Twelve.* *TWELVE YEARS!*" Victoria's voice slid up in pitch and volume, ending just below a scream. *Gotta watch it, don't want to wake the old bear.* Heavy air started moving across her bare arms. She saw gathering clouds out of the corner of her eye.

"Victoria." Celeste's voice was cool. "Are you certain you want to tell me about this?" Her Boston accent sounded more formal, more pronounced than usual.

What?! "Celeste, I just gotta tell someone or I'll pop. I haven't told anyone this in years!!" Now Victoria could hear the whine in her voice.

"Perhaps a cool bath with those nice lemon crystals, dear. Yes, yes, that's just what you need. Don't you think that would be lovely, Victoria?" She imagined Celeste's fingers busy twisting the string of Japanese pearls around her throat as she spoke.

Damn! Cry, and you cry alone. Reject him once, and he freezes me out. Victoria wanted to scream. Saturated hot air mixed with cooler streams, like warm oatmeal and cool milk, and blew across her arms. She heard a soft boom and saw small flashes of light from the corner of her eye; she wondered if it was thunder or firecrackers from the parking lot ten floors below.

"Celeste," she said in a detached voice, "Celeste. Please. I really need to talk with you. Maybe, maybe, can I come down after all?"

"Of course, my dear. Perhaps a nice Campari and tonic about eight o'clock." Her voice was bright and social again. "I'll get the ice bucket ready."

The receiver hummed in Victoria's ear. Hanging up, she stashed the phone under the table. *Might need that later*, she thought. She stood up as a streak of lightning and loud clap of thunder made her and Tripper jump. *Oh, hell, it's gonna rain like all get out.* She slid the door open, and scooped up her dog. Another deafening thunder clap chased them into the living room.

As the woman and dog dropped into the recliner, the television, lights, and air conditioning died in unison, leaving the apartment hot, dark, close and deathly still. Seconds later the bedroom door jerked open. Another flash of lightning threw blue-white light on Neal's half-clad, half-asleep, double-sized body.

"What the hell!" Neal lunged into the living room. "What the hell is going on?! And why is that damned balcony door open? Close the damned thing before we drown," he demanded. A furious, instant rain shot into the apartment, soaking the carpet and wetting the walls. "Never mind, I'll do it my own damned self."

Still groggy from sleep, he held his hand along the wall for balance as he shuffled down the hallway to close the sliding door. Victoria was immediately behind him, and Tripper was twisting around with storm-fed excitement. Just before slamming the door, Neal noticed his cigar cutter and lighter outside, unprotected from the torrents of water. "Aw, shit," he muttered and pulled the door open wide enough to step out in the blinding rain.

Tripper raced past Victoria, circled Neal's left ankle and headed back inside. Neal grabbed his gear, and pivoted as another lightning bolt sizzled. Startled, he lurched forward. His bound foot caught in a hole in the carpet. He fell headlong toward the open door.

Without stopping to plan, Victoria yanked the door shut and liberated Tripper from his leash. Neal's head hit the heavy door frame. Red blood, white rain, and blue lightning washed his body.

Neal staggered backward. His arms spun. He grabbed for the chair and missed. His right foot snagged in the telephone cord as he tried to catch himself against the railing.

Weak aluminum failed under his massive moving weight. Neal shot out over the edge of the concrete, a long arc over the edge of the balcony, down and away from the sky and clouds and broken railing.

The rain stopped when Neal did.

A long moment later the AC, lights, and television flickered on.

Victoria turned to her little dog and said, "Now, Tripper, why don't we go and make some yummy toast in that shiny toaster while I make us some new plans for Independence Day?"

St. Pete Bay

*Quebec House Apartment Building, Washington, DC,
Late March, 1999*

"Angie, dear, why don't we sit at the table by the window, wouldn't that be too salubrious?" Sheila Fitzgerald Short and Angie Sparks sat at a small table, snugged up against a long picture window, in Sheila's Quebec House apartment. "Shall I be mother? Hibiscus tea, they say, is good for blood pressure."

"What's that, Sheila? Is that one of those British things you like to say, because we're having tea?" Angie gave Sheila a toothy smile, and waited for her to pour the tea.

"Yes, I suppose it is. Sometimes," Sheila said, as she sat down and smoothed back her graying hair, "sometimes even *I* think I read too much!" Sheila gave a small laugh that ended in a cough. "Oh, dear, must be allergies, all those falling leaves," and drank some tea.

Outside—Sheila's window faced Connecticut Avenue through a stand of trees—drizzle grayed the mid-afternoon light. Water globs returned to earth from their holiday in the sky. Aged leaves ran to ground.

"Anyway," Angie said, and turned toward the window. Rain shadows tucked themselves into her coco-butter skin. "Now that I'm... well, *not working*, I can spend more time visiting. You're just one floor over, and one floor down." She gave a deep, deep sigh. "Seems like the fall rain started early this year, don't you think? Suits me perfectly."

Sheila reached across the table and put her hand on top of her friend's wrist. "Please, can you tell me what happened? I, I have a special reason to ask, not just to be solicitous."

Angie scrunched her face at the last word. "Not too sure what you mean, but I can tell you mean well. So," she drew a deep breath, "here it is."

As she started to speak, Sheila offered her a salute to America: a homemade red, white, and blue scone. "Two weeks ago, Friday afternoon, there I was, sitting at my Reception Desk, getting ready to leave work. O'Johns calls me into his office, Perry the office manager was there. Looking very Howdy-Doody, as always. He always goes along with O'Johns. So I can smell something is up, not just O'Johns' god-awful smells-like-feet aftershave. Anyways," she took a large bite of scone and washed it down.

"Anyways, O'Johns tells me that they are reorganizing and my skills don't fit in the department any more! My *skills*, like they're *separate* from *me*, Sheila! So he says, in kind of a rush, here's some papers, sign them—he makes it sound like I don't have a choice—and be quick because they have a taxi waiting, don't want to cost the firm any extra money."

Sheila sputtered, gripped her friend's hand again. "What bald temerity! And for a law firm to do that kind of thing!! How long were you there, dear?"

"Fifteen years." Angie set her cup down in its saucer, strongly, deliberately. "Fifteen years. Perfect record. Just about ready to retire, full retirement age too. That's their pattern, pull down the dying leaves on their trees before they fall." The rain pattern continued across her face. "And then Margo-Lynn Malinger, that *maroon* in Human Resources, pokes her ugly donkey head in the door and frog-marches me to my Reception Desk. Gave me a box and said put all my things in it. Then, *then* said in her fanny-smooching way that I should think it was a *blessing in disguise*. You're good with words, Sheila, what's a word that rhymes with *bitch*?"

Sheila stood, walked to her desk in the corner, and came back with a letter she put in front of Angie. "I got this in yesterday's post. It's from those miscreants at your, your *former*, law firm."

"Sorry, Sheila, I just can't focus on it right now..."

Sheila sat, strongly, deliberately. "I'll be happy to give you a summary. It *demands* that I visit the office of O'Johns and Richards, and insinuates that they will take legal action if I don't show up. In two days. Not a syllable as to what or why, just lots of references to statutes and other legal falderal."

"Oh, Sheila, be careful, you know how—"

"The letter was condescending, fatuous, arrogant, patronizing, freighted with *menace*, positively *freighted with menace...*" Sheila stood, taut, rigid with fury. "That letter, on top of what they did to you..."

Angie stood, and put a gentle hand on her friend's shoulder. "Sheila, sweetie. Sweetie. You are preaching to the preacher."

Sheila relaxed. "Oh, please forgive me, Angie! It is you, really, who are the victim of their viciousness. I have a vivid imagination, thinking they want me to take part in their intrigue against you. Please forgive my scree, my imprecations." She sat down again, and motioned her friend to sit too.

"Oh, no, I think I know that look on your face. All determined and all. *What* are you thinking, Sheila?"

"Well, to quote a famous playwright, 'The first thing we do, let's kill all the lawyers.' He didn't mean it, but *we* do. Figuratively, *verbally,* of course. Of course." She pushed her glasses back against the bridge of her nose, and looked intently at her friend. "What about unemployment? A nice age-discrimination or hostile work environment case? I read so much about that in the *Washington Post.*"

"Yes, well, they don't tell you what a mess DC unemployment is. Went that way years ago, never again. And a lawsuit? As you would say, Sheila: balderdash! The very least they would do is stall until I'm too poor to keep suing, whether I'm right or wrong. They don't seem to give a hang about bad publicity." Angie smashed a blueberry into a cherry with her fork.

Sheila stood and looked out at falling leaves, pushed out of their trees by the heavy rain. She turned back to her friend. "What would you say, Angie, if we all—all of us here in the Quebec House, your *residential family,* so to speak—if we all held a rally, a protest, brought public censure to bear on O'Johns and his firm? You know we all love you here. And we can't just sit by and watch them practically *kill* you!"

Angie looked alarmed. "No, oh please, no, Sheila." She took a gulp of tea. "Here's how it is. Or was. My desk, the Reception Desk, was right outside his office. And he must think I can't hear, that he has some special protective layer or something. Anyway, for *years* I heard all the nasty double-deals he was up to, usually with Richards and Cooks. My luck, he'd find a way to buy the Quebec House, kick us all out, tear it down, and put up a museum. To himself, of course."

"I learned a few things about lawyers from fighting to clear Jameson's name. Let me see what his devious mind has cooked up. I just hate to see you taken hostage by your own good nature. More tea?"

* * * * *

Matty

Matthew O'Johns was short, thick of waist, thin of hair, and had teeth that stuck out like guns from a blockhouse. He sat at a conference table opposite Mrs. Sheila Fitzgerald Short in the law office of O'Johns and Richards, squirreled away in one of the many toasters-with-windows buildings on K Street. The room smelled of stale, cheap aftershave.

"Thank you for coming in so quickly, Mrs. Short. *Vita brevis*, as they say. That means life is short."

Sheila flinched. "Yes, I know—"

"My friends call me Matty, Matty O'Johns." He slid his business card toward Mrs. Short. She did not pick it up. He opened the file folder in front of him and added, "I'll get to the point quickly." His smile was years away from his eyes.

Mrs. Short blinked, hiding for a moment her faded blue eyes behind thick, rimless glasses. "Thank you too much." She could not resist adding, "I'm certain you don't mean to spend an unnecessary moment with me." *Though I just spent forty-five minutes in your lobby, waiting for you.* A closed-mouth smile sent her message across the table.

"It seems Mr. Robespierre, your neighbor, died early this year."

"Seems?" Sheila raised one eyebrow. Another signal sent.

"He was a client of ours, of O'Johns and Richards, for many years. He'd probably agree with that *brevis* part, right?" Matty O'Johns looked up from the papers in front of him, and attempted a smile. "Did you know him well?"

"No," she said, and let the answer hang for a moment. "Albert was my upstairs neighbor, we became friendly over the many years we lived in the Quebec House." She shifted back in her seat, and stared intently at him. *Toad*, she thought, *you are an absolute, unctuous toad.* "No, I didn't know him well. Why do you ask?"

O'Johns cleared his throat, and looked down again. "Just routine, Mrs. Short. But the reason I asked you here is to have you sign some papers. Some legal papers," he added.

Condescending toad. She pulled herself upright again, never letting her gaze waiver. "Regarding?" *I wish I had a nice beverage right now, something strong enough to neutralize this odious oaf. Something to wash down a nice cigarette.*

"In short, Mrs. Shor—" he stopped himself just in time. "He named you in his will. He left you his condominium in St. Petersburg."

Don't, just don't *say Flor—*

"In Florida, of course." He aimed his dental artillery at her.

"What? Please repeat yourself. *Not* the Florida information." She launched her other eyebrow at him.

"It seems he—" he began, "I mean Mr. Robespierre *was* a dual citizen of Canada and the United States. He lived in Penetanguishene in the summer and lived in DC when Canada got too cold. He was head of the Costume Department for the Canadian Opera Company, but retired many years ago. The company didn't have much money, so they paid him with thousands of costumes they no longer needed."

Ah, those costumes... that explains so *much!* Sheila thought. *I thought all those strange clothes in his apartment were just a quirk, taking up so much space he had to sleep in his living room...*

"Kind of a *quid pro quo*. That means—"

Sheila did not completely suppress a groan.

"That means that aside from the legal complications of dual citizenship, we have had to sell his collection. Our fees, you know." Then, looking smug, he added, "We managed to get quite a good price for them, as some of them have become antiques. So we can waive our usual fees. Got to pay for my new beach house after all, the Outer Banks isn't cheap." Matty O'Johns smirked at his own joke. Sheila did not smile.

Blood, blood, even from a dead turnip. I believe someone *said* something *like that, or they should have.*

"Mr. O'Johns, you were saying about the condo...?"

"Yes, yes, he managed to buy a place in St. Petersburg many years ago, when prices were low. *Carpe diem*, as they— well, anyway, it's a modest place, but the neighborhood has become quite desirable. It's a 55-plus community. And it's yours. We want you to sign all the paperwork today, so we can close the file."

Sheila blinked several times. "Florida?" she asked. "So far away..."

"Yes, it is," said O'Johns, "and it overlooks the bay. Vinca Terrace. Condo 417 is all yours, just as soon as you sign this pile of papers. *Veni vidi vici Vinca*, eh?" He laughed at his own joke. "Oh, and the good news is that we have a branch office in Tampa, right across the bay, for all your legal needs!"

*   *   *   *   *

Immediately after Mrs. Short left the conference room, Matty O'Johns jabbed buttons on the speakerphone to call his office in Tampa. After a few rings, he heard Brian Richards, his law partner, answer the phone.

"Richards! Matty here," O'Johns yelled into the speakerphone on the conference room table.

"Yes, Matty, I know it's you. And for God's sake, no need to yell. All the phone lines are working between DC and Tampa."

"Vinca Terrace. That deal still on? The one you and Cooks are working on?"

"Yes," said Brian Richards. "We should be able to buy the Vinca in about a year, tear it down, and sell the land to the city about three months later."

For no one to see, O'Johns flashed a smile. Flecks of dried spit crouched in the corners of his mouth. "And the city will still buy at the price we talked about?"

"No changes here. They really want to see the bayfront lined with museums. Bye-bye Vinca baby!" Richards made a booming sound and snorted. "The city didn't even ask where all those old folks will go when we demo the building."

"I have a few destinations if they can't think of any! And you thought it sounded crazy, right, to use the whole St. Pete Bay thing to get the city to turn against the sweet old folks!! The whole name change thing must really rankle City Hall types."

"Like sand in a bathing suit," said Richards. "Like sand in a bathing suit." He gave another laughing snort.

O'Johns stood up and leaned over the speakerphone, as if it were a confidant. "Just so long as they don't know we're paying some of those old codgers to agitate, that's all. If you can call six months of free medications paying them. You did pick codgers about ready to ... well, who were pretty far *advanced*, right?"

"Oh yeah. Those senior shills, you could knock them over without trying."

"No way they could trace this back to us?"

"No, we'll take this one to our graves." O'Johns grunted his approval.

"Oh, and take Cooks with you."

"That moron! Anyways, he's in the Broken Bone office."

"Close it! We only opened that dust hole for the D'Arcangelos. And to find something to do with that fool Cooks. We can do that from here."

"But Matty—"

"Come on, Brian, we've talked about this. He looks like everyone's chubby uncle, smiles a lot—that keeps them from getting too curious or upset. Not the best lawyer, not even good, but he is a good, crazy distraction. Kind of an ugly magician's assistant. And remember how he helped with the Skydown Terrace mess? We got a tidy bundle from that."

"All right, all right. Consider the deal done. Easy money. Easy *big* money. For us, that is! You know us: do or die."

"Oh, yes. Gotta renovate that new beach house."

O'Johns hit the disconnect button, sat down, and gave himself a big old hug.

*   *   *   *   *

St. Petersburg, Florida,
April, 1999

"Celeste, darling, move a little closer to the window. The view is quite salubrious!" Mrs. Sheila Short leaned her shoulder against her friend—her best friend for practically ever—and pointed through the front window of their double-decker bus. The mid-morning sun showed St. Petersburg at its best. Their front seats on the upper deck of the bus let them drink in the beauty, as promised by the tour bus advertisements.

"Sheila, you are in for a surprise just beyond this hill. I believe you will see how far we have come from dear old Dorchester."

Sheila gave a small cough. "I didn't know St. Petersburg had any hills to speak of, so I'm eager to—" Mrs. Celeste Lobosco interrupted her friend with a small nudge and aimed a finger out the front window.

Their tour bus crested a small hill on Central Avenue, and began its slow descent to the bay, now in full view. The two long-time friends were silent for a few moments.

"My," said Sheila, "it's even nicer than those Cinerama™ movies we had at the Uptown Theater! Quite like the Mediterranean."

In front of them, the bay was clear and the sky was sunny. Celeste and the other tour bus passengers saw small, sparkling waves. Sheila saw ebullient sun splinters on vacation from the sky.

The overhead speaker crackled as the girlish voice of their tour guide piped up, "Ladies and Gentlemen, ahead is an almost forgotten part of St. Petersburg. Usually, the Gulf of Mexico gets all the visitors and all the attention, but we have in front of us the reason the first visitors chose this spot. The mouth of the bay is protected from the Gulf, out of sight and bad weather. The bay, though, is spacious enough for large sailing ships."

Their guide was warming up to her subject. "Looking across the water, you can see the city of Tampa. Mistakenly, many assume that all the water here is Tampa Bay. But it is not!" Her voice rose. "Not by a long shot! This, in front of you, is and always will be *St. Petersburg* Bay!" Her voice got louder, climbed higher still. "There is just NO reason for them to grab the name for themselves, I swear. What bullies! That damn Tampa... The Bay is dead, long live the Bay!!" Scuffling sounds from the lower deck, and then the microphone went dead.

"My dear, that was a bit unusual, yes? I can't imagine what that was all about." Celeste toyed with the Japanese pearls around her neck.

"Undoubtedly. I did not realize our tour came with an epanalepsis." *But somehow*, she thought, *somehow I like the name St. Petersburg Bay. To answer the age-old question, there's quite a bit in a name.* She leaned forward to peer at the water through her thick prescription sunglasses. "Do you think seven maids with seven mops swept this for half a year?" Sheila laughed at her own joke; Celeste checked the clasp on her sweater set.

"Ladies and gentlemen," a male voice addressed them from the speaker, "we apologize for any ... inconvenience. Today was Karen's first day as your tour guide, and she ... must have first day jitters. Yes, yes, that's right." He paused. "Ahead is *Tampa* Bay, home to about four million residents. The city's name most likely came from the Calusa Native Americans, and it means sticks of fire—a possible reference to the many lightning strikes in this area."

"Good heavens," said Sheila, "that sounds perilous!"

The replacement guide continued his spiel. "Tampa Bay is Florida's largest open-water estuary, with more than 200 species of fish. In 1917, the Corps of Engineers dredged a channel from the mouth of Tampa Bay to the Port of Tampa, instantly making the city an important shipping center." The guide continued to tell them about the area as the bus turned north along Bayshore Drive.

"Look to your left, dear, you'll see your new home. Your building is between North and South Straub Parks." Celeste nodded her chin to their left. "And there's that splendid Bicentennial Water Sculpture. Picture yourself sitting in the park, reading under one of those shady banyan trees. And the parks are a stone's throw from the condo."

Set back from Bayshore Drive, sweeping along an entire block, pale pink with periwinkle trim: it was Vinca Terrace. The four story building was unassuming in its flat-roof, motel-style design. *The walkways make it look so public like a frog, like it used to zigzag then got snapped straight. But it's mine, my new home.* Leaning out from the center of the top-floor railing, a cantilevered flag brushed all-American colors on to the bay breeze. She squinted as she counted condo doors to find her new home on the top floor. She could see the Vinca's flat roof, with its army of air conditioners and its squat turbine shafts, like aluminum lunar landers. *I believe I will miss the lovely roof of the Quebec House.*

Sheila moved closer to the window beside her and pulled on the elbow of her friend's sweater. "Ah, there it is. It looks too good to be true. The realtor said he'd give me the keys tomorrow morning, and I'll move in as soon as my furniture arrives."

Home, Sheila thought, *that's almost a strange idea to me. Boston was all about marrying Jameson, Washington was me and raising my son. St. Petersburg is all mine, I suppose. Lawks-a-mussy, am I having some odd identity crisis?*

"This was an excellent idea, Celeste, taking a tourist's view of my new home town. How far are we from your place?"

"Hmm, I believe Skydown Terrace is about three miles, as the gull flies. We're not chock-a-block neighbors, not the way we were in Dorchester, but we are just across town. My husband simply loves to drive, so you'll see me and Joseph in your guest parking spot regularly."

"And you are certain your upstairs neighbor doesn't mind a temporary lodger in her place?"

"Oh tosh, not at all! Victoria said you can stay in her place as long as you like. The top floor has a wonderful view, though the place is dreadfully small."

Celeste continued, "Poor Victoria, I know she puts on a brave front, but losing her husband that way must have been terrible. He tumbled all the way down to the parking lot, I've been told."

Sheila's mind flashed a picture of Jameson, her long-dead husband, but time had dulled her interior PowerPoint show.

"Sheila," said Celeste in a confidential tone of voice, "Joseph was so upset he wouldn't go out on our balcony for weeks, especially near the railing. He says it's a wrought-iron lightning rod! He positively *flinches* when he hears thunder! Anyway, I will miss Victoria. We enjoyed so many cocktail hours together. She seemed so eager to go home to Broken Bone, I hope she's happy there."

"And the Salvador Dalí Museum, Celeste? How do I get to it from the Vinca?"

"The museum is a short walk down Third Street. How wonderful that they want you as one of their docents! But here's some delightful news. The museum will be moving soon, so it will be a ten-minute walk—I know how you hate to drive—just down Bayshore Drive."

"Such a pity there aren't more museums along the waterfront. It seems an ideal location."

The tour bus rolled northward. Bayshore Drive curved outward like a fish hook, leaving the grand Vinoy hotel, peachy pink in the morning sun, anchored behind it. On, up, around, the tour bus rolled and spiraled through St. Petersburg. Each palm-fanned park, each bayou, each reminder that this was a special place: all seemed to Sheila to be urged to the surface of the earth by a warm, glorious force.

She sat back in her seat and fanned herself with the tour bus brochure.

"Lawks-a-mussy, Celeste, I believe I'm a bit weary from these wonders we wander through. Shall we stop for a bit of brunch?" Sheila's voice was thin, raspy, and she felt a soft sweat of exertion on her upper lip.

"Yes, of course. Just ahead is the Rache Café that Joseph and I enjoy. We'll have some tea and one of their fine cold dishes, then we can call it a morning." Celeste looked closely at her friend. "Perhaps we can call it a *day* after that. After all, we *are* senior citizens. Or at least in the tea time of our life!"

The two old friends laughed, but Sheila's chuckle ended with a prolonged cough.

Sheila held up a thin hand to stop the concern she could see on her friend's face. "Tomorrow. I go to the Respiratory Clinic tomorrow. They'll tell me I need a stronger inhaler, remind me that emphysema is chronic. Their news is coals to Newcastle, I tell them, but they clearly have no education beyond the medical."

They were quiet for a few moments. "You know, Celeste, my philosophy is that life is an oubliette, and that—"

"Oubliette, dear? My vocabulary can usually keep up, but..."

"So sorry. An oubliette is a prison cell. Its only opening is in its ceiling. So life is an oubliette, and the only way out of this oubliette is *up!*" Sheila patted her friend's hand.

"Very well, I'm certain you know best. The café is at the next stop, and I'm feeling a bit peckish, as you would say." Celeste snugged her sweater a little closer, hiding her worried look in their slow flurry to exit the bus.

*   *   *   *   *

417 Vinca Terrace, St. Petersburg, Florida,
One week later

The ringing telephone brought Sheila in from her balcony. She made her way through half-unpacked boxes and discomposed furniture to the kitchen peninsula as quickly as she could. She picked up the canary-yellow receiver of her wall phone.

"Hello, hello," she said, her voice breathy from her mild exertion.

"Mrs. Short? I hope I'm not disturbing you. This is Arlene Tyler, in 124." The voice was loud; Sheila moved the receiver away from her ear.

"Why, hello, Arlene. I'm—"

"Mrs. Short? I'm sorry, I don't hear too well. Is that you? Let me fiddle with my phone." Sheila's receiver squawked.

Sheila paused for a moment, then said "Hello? Hello? This is Mrs. Short. Can you hear me any better?" Sheila spoke at a higher pitch with as much volume as she thought appropriate.

"Oh, why of course, Mrs. Short. Anyway, this is Arlene Tyler, I live downstairs. I hope I'm not disturbing you."

"Oh, not at all Ar—"

"Wonderful. Anyway, I'm calling to welcome you to the building. The Condo Board appointed me the official

Welcome Lady just last week, you know, at the most recent board meeting. They told us to expect you."

"Well, that's very gracious. I really appreciate—"

"Okay, then, thanks Mrs. Short. Hope to see you at the next board meeting." The line went dead.

And I, Queen of Sweden, do humbly accept your gracious welcome, Sheila thought and headed back out to her balcony. Nestled among moving boxes, Sheila found the house-warming chair Celeste had given her. "I imagine you'll spend many hours sitting out here reading," Celeste told her, "and I want you to be comfortable." The chair, an over-sized saucer on a circular base, dwarfed Sheila. "And Joseph and I have had many discussions as to whether this is rattan or wicker."

Sheila sat and looked through her balcony's screen at the St. Petersburg western skyline; four floors below, tourists hunted parking spaces on Beach Drive. Cars made soft sounds, insinuations, hissing rumors, indirect imitations of the bay's shushing waters.

Lifting a frosty, sweating cocktail glass, Sheila made a toast in the air and said, "God bless you, Albert Maximilien Robespierre." *There I was, ready to retire, not a clue as to what or how to proceed. Or maybe I should toast to Deus ex machina?* She idly picked at the palm leaves in the cushion's floral pattern.

I believe I'm going to like it here, all thousand square feet of my own Toad Hall. Dear Virginia Woolf, if you are looking down on me right now, is this what you meant by a room of one's own?

"But I am dithering," she said to her new chair, screen, balcony, condo, and the world at large. "Time to get domestic. Now, where did the realtor say they keep the laundry room?"

*   *   *   *   *

Watch Your Legs

Sheila backed out of her condo, pulling her laundry cart as she closed her door, and made her way along the outdoor walkway to the fourth-floor lobby. She clutched her coin purse of quarters and rang for the elevator. From the corner of her eye she could see the condo's flag twitching in the tangy on-shore breeze. Beyond the railing and the flag was the bay, a trampoline for the early afternoon sun. Sheila was hypnotized by the soft breeze, the warm sun, and a hint of hibiscus. Still dreamy as the elevator door opened, she gathered her cart and coins, then was startled to hear a husky voice behind her.

"Here comes Peg, watch your legs." With a toot of its horn, a scooter slid around her and slipped into the open elevator. The scooter turned along the back wall and stopped.

"Come on in, honey, there's plenty of room for all of us! This is my shiny new Peugeot Scoot'Elec. All 'lectric and all. Dazzlin', ain't it?" The woman on the scooter looked up at Sheila. "Come on in honey. Tempis is fugiting, and these elevators are real, real slow."

Sheila and her laundry joined the woman and her scooter, and elevator door slid shut. "Three?"

"Yes, yes, please."

"We don't stand on formalities around here, honey. I'm Peg. Live in 426. You must be that new gal that moved into 417. Hope I didn't get you with my scooter. Here comes Peg, watch your legs, I always say." Peg tooted the horn again. "Sure does sound loud in here, doesn't it?"

Gal? Sheila thought *I haven't been called that in decades. Not that seventy is considered old, not these days.*

Peg twisted around to look up at Sheila again. She— Peg—was a smallish, plumpish, nice-ish looking woman with a roundish face, over-dyed black hair, and deeply weathered skin.

"Sheila. Sheila Short." Sheila's fine-boned hand shook Peg's fingers, her swollen knuckles making a full handshake unlikely.

"Well, Sheila, you'll do real well here." Sheila smiled at her encouragement. "A young gal like you..." Sheila's smile disappeared. "Married, honey?" Sheila shook her head.

Sometimes, Sheila thought, *it's better to be alone than to wish you were.*

The elevator door opened. Sheila rolled her cart out into the lobby. As the elevator door began to close, Peg said, "Hope to see you at the rally, doll! Or maybe at the pool!!" She gave her horn another toot. The door closed the conversation.

The sign on a louvered door beside the elevator was unnecessary; Sheila could hear sloshing machines and smell fabric softener. She opened the door into a small, brightly lit room crammed with washers and dryers. *A utilitarian utopia*, she thought. *Happy pistons that run on quarters.*

All but two of the washing machines were in use. Sheila read the directions, loaded her laundry and detergent, and pumped in a large batch of quarters.

* * * * *

Arch Friends

Kitted out in a modest mauve bathing suit, soft maroon terry cloth robe, straw hat, sandals, and clad in fragrant sun block: it was Sheila Fitzgerald Short, making her debut at the Vinca's swimming pool. "Even if you can't swim," Celeste had advised her, "you must make an appearance at the pool. Chlorine is the social life blood of your building. And remember, you are a comparative *ingénue*."

The pool was tucked along the south side of the Vinca. A buffer of viburnum hedges shielded residents from passersby. A pergola ran the length of the pool, offering shade to a few shady lawn chairs and lounges as protection from killer radiation. Sheila found the deepest shade she could in the mid-afternoon sun, leaned back in her chaise lounge, and started to re-read *Orlando: A Biography*.

Over her book, she saw a few sun-baked bodies in the pool. On the other side of the water, bearing the brunt of the sun, sat a dozen or so seniors whose bodies made peace with their age. Walkers, scooters, and canes were resting by the hedges. She noticed a few of the men had faded tattoos that marked them as former sailors. The women wore their extra flesh as proof of their courage to bear children. They lay on their lounges, some puffy soufflés, some deflated.

Conversation drifted up from the pool to make small clouds in the sky. The swimmers commented on where the sun made the pool nice and warm, and lamented how chilly the bay breeze was today.

A dark shadow bookmarked Sheila's reading. She tented her hand across her forehead and looked up at the figure blocking most of the sun.

"Well, what do you think? Pretty nifty, yes?" the silhouette asked, pointing to its forehead. "I mean, they match, right?" A trim woman, clad in a bright green bathing suit, eased herself into the lounge beside Sheila.

"I beg your pardon?"

"Sorry, I thought I saw you looking, earlier. You must be new here."

"Forgive me if I seem nonplussed." The woman stared at her blankly. "I mean, I don't know what you mean."

"My fault entirely. I'm Clara." Clara stretched out, favoring her elbow. Sheila could see deep scars across her new friend's right arm, and a large bandage on her elbow. "Clara Davies. 402. I think we're floor mates. You must be the woman who just moved into 417."

Clara reached across with her left arm and held it out for Sheila to shake hands. Sheila took it gently and gave Clara's hand a squeeze. Clara's hand smelled strongly of a bad perfume knock-off.

"Sorry, bum elbow. Fell off my platform shoes. Six surgeries. Six. Want to see the scars?" She started to lift her bandage.

"Oh, no, no. Thank you. I wouldn't want to interfere with your healing."

"Keeps me from working. Nearly thirty-five years, now I'm just no good." Clara removed an orange bandana from her bleached hair and draped it across her face. "Better than sun block, I swear. Can't stand the stuff myself. So you're new here, right? Worked doing eyebrows my whole life. Just did my own, for once, wanted to be sure they matched. Started my own business, over at Tyrone Square. Arch Friends. Heard of it? Just my own little joke, not sure anyone else got it. Just got trained on filling them in, eyebrows, with tattoos. Then this damned elbow."

As she spoke, the bandana stuck to her thick lipstick; she blew hard to remove it. "Even had to let my assistant go. That Tiffany, best little helper. Great at keeping the wax at just the right temperature. No good at other stuff. Think she quit working altogether, took up with some roofer. I mean, that skill isn't exactly portable. Or maybe *she* became a roofer, I can't quite recall. Or does she make hats now? All this medication."

"How nice, I mean how sad... I mean..."

Clara removed her sun protection, wrapped it around her hair, and stood up. She looked at Sheila's book cover. "Oh, *Orlando*. Didn't realize they wrote a book about the place. Heard they postponed the rally until next Friday. Are you going?"

Before Sheila could respond, Clara cupped her hands around her Inca-Pinca lips and yelled into the water, "Hey, Ruth, how's your knee? Hope they gave you a good one this time." A cylindrical woman in a flowered bathing cap waved to Clara and nodded.

Clara turned back and said to Sheila, in a quieter voice, "Damn lily ponders, clogging up the whole pool. That's what I call them. They just grab a noodle, wade into the middle of the pool, and bob up and down talking to their friends. How are we supposed to get in our laps? Guess I'd better take a walk instead."

Before she could walk away, Sheila said, "Clara, just a moment please. Please. Just *what* is the rally about? I keep hearing it mentioned, but no one—"

"The bay, of course, the bay," she said over her shoulder, waving goodbye with her good arm.

*   *   *   *   *

Happy Hour

Celeste looked around Sheila's condo. "You did all this in just one month? I simply cannot believe you haven't lived here for years! I didn't even notice your tiled floors before. And that palm tree tatouage really makes the place. *Very Florida!*" She lifted her cocktail glass in Sheila's direction—sitting on the rattan sofa beside the wicker arm chair—and said, "Here's to a *bon vivant* life at the Vinca—and your wonderful invention, the *Vinca-tini!*"

"It's my own negus for the Vinca Terrace: a heavenly concoction of rum and a powdered fruit drink," she confided to Celeste.

A bay breeze, like a friendly spirit, slid through the screen door, past the tropical furniture, along the peach-tinted walls, past Sheila's new teak dining room table, out to the balcony to play with the Heavenly Blue Morning Glories that were learning to climb the screen.

"Celeste," Sheila said, taking a small bite of the smoked oysters on a Ritz she was serving her guest, "Celeste, I do have one uneasiness in this paradise." She tried to look over the top of her glasses at her life-long friend.

Celeste dabbed the corner of her mouth with a cocktail napkin, and looked at Sheila. "Yes?"

"Well," she said, smoothing imaginary wrinkles out of her new heather gray sweatpants, "yesterday I saw a man walking around with a teddy bear wrapped in foil, strapped on like a papoose." She gave her new slouch socks a tug, purchased along with her sweatpants that morning from Salvation Army. Celeste had told her that it was *the* shabby chic store to be seen at. "It appears that the Vinca is a bit of real estate right out of Alice in Wonderland."

"Wonderland? Oh, tosh," said Celeste, and relaxed back into the floral cushions. "Tosh and tutty-kins." She hiccupped, then poured herself another Vinca-tini from the carafe on the bamboo end table. Her eyes rambled.

"My dear, you simply can't imagine the oddness of my fellow Vinca—*Vinkettes?*—but you take my meaning. Simply odd."

"Florida is very proud of its eccentrics, you know," said Celeste between bites of her appetizer and sips of her drink. "I suppose that's a quirk of its own, but I have lived here too long to be certain." She reached for another refill.

"Yes, but—" She was interrupted by a knock on her screen door, followed by a thump, and a second thump. Then a loud toot. "Lawks-a-mussy, who or what..." Sheila got up to answer the door.

Through the screen she could see a bottle-blonde woman standing behind a dark-haired woman on a scooter. "Sheila, girl, it's us. Me and Clara." Peg tooted the horn on her scooter again to prove her point. "C'mon, you're going to the rally aren't ya? We're getting ready right now. Want us to come in and give you a hand?" Peg backed up her scooter, pushing Clara hard against the railing.

"Like, yoowwwch. Lady. Get a license for that thing!" A moment's pause, and then a small gale of girlish laughter.

Sheila opened her screen door, but not wide enough to let in her visitors. "Oh, I'm so sorry, ladies, I have company at the moment. Maybe we can join you a little later?"

Celeste bumped along the front hall like an inebriated pinball, then put up a hand to steady herself as she stood behind Sheila. "Oh, hello. Celeste Lobosco here. What's this I hear about a rally? Joseph and I often go to Daytona to watch the *bicycle* ral—"

Peg tooted her horn again. "Sorry, finger must have slipped. Anyways, we just came by to let Sheila know the rally starts in about twenty minutes in the first floor lobby. Tooda-loo!" she said, and headed her scooter down the walkway to the elevator; Clara was right behind her, waving her good arm over her shoulder.

Sheila closed her screen door, locked it, and then closed her inner door. She locked that too. Celeste tottered back into her chair.

Sheila sighed, and sat down. "What is all this about a rally? All I have heard is 'the bay, it's about the bay', whatever they mean by that."

Celeste giggled, and guzzled again. "Oh, Sheila, you *read* far too much! It's all over the local news. Rebellion has been fomented, so to speak. Or did they say fermented? Well, in either case, they want to rename Tampa Bay to Chesapeake Bay. I mean, I mean St. Petersburg Bay. Seems the Vinca is leading the way for the name change, in the vanguard as they say. When they're not saying things like fermented." Celeste began to slide down into the cushions. She sat bolt upright when Sheila said,

"Shall we go? Joseph won't be here for at least another hour. What the heck and why not anyways?!" She gave Celeste her an impish look and headed for her bedroom. "Be right out. Help yourself to some more refreshments."

*   *   *   *   *

Rally Round the Flag

As they rode the elevator down to the first floor lobby, Sheila and Celeste could hear a commotion. Above the noise, Sheila asked, "Did you notice if Mr. Simmons has taken in the flag already? It's not sunset yet, but given the convocation in the lobby ... ."

Celeste was leaning against the elevator wall. "Simmons?" she murmured.

"He lives two doors down from me. Barry Simmons. I believe I mentioned him." *But I didn't tell you he's tall, rugged yet refined.* Sheila pictured his full head of silvery hair, Lyle Waggoner tan, and broad smile with teeth like Tony Curtis. "He puts out the flag every sunrise, and takes it in at sunset. Ever since Mr. Othello died last fall. I heard *all* about it at the pool. *Overheard*, really."

"Somebody's got a boy friend, somebody's got a boyfriend," Celeste chanted until the elevator door opened. The noise in the lobby drowned out her taunt.

On Bayshore Drive, traffic crawled. Horns honked. On the lawn that separated the Vinca from the street, a camerawoman from WSPB-TV was setting up remote broadcasting equipment. In the parking lot, cars were competing to arrive and leave. A few food trucks were parked along the edges of the driveway; the pizza truck seemed especially popular. The sidewalk was thick with people in bathing suits, office suits, and a few clown suits. Some of them carried signs they waved with gusto.

Sheila and Celeste could hear the chants. "Hey, hey, what do you say, it's St. Pete not Tampa Bay!," and "Hoo hoo, boo hoo, smile and pout, St. Pete's in and Tampa's out!"

"Heaven forefend," Sheila said. She reached for the inhaler in her purse and gave herself a bracing blast.

A loud screech brought the crowd to a quiet standstill. Straddling the lawn and the parking lot, wearing a baseball cap and fumbling with a bullhorn: it was Peg. "Ladies and Gentlemen, welcome to the first St. Pete Bay rally!" Peg screamed into the bullhorn. "We have a lawyer here from Tampa Bay that—" she was briefly drowned out by boos from the crowd. "A lawyer who wants to speak to us about changing the name. *Not* changing, if you ask me!" A loud cheer went up. Peg tooted her scooter's horn for silence. "Standing in our top floor lobby is Danny Cooks, from the law firm of—what's that? Oh, sorry, got the name wrong, whatever—we have Davy Cross from O'Johns and Richards. He has a few words for us. Take it away, Danny. Sorry, I mean Davy." A rotund man with a rotund grin leaned over the fourth-floor railing, with a bullhorn in one chubby hand and the American flag in the other.

Celeste tugged on Sheila's arm. "Sweetie, I'm feeling a bit thirsty. I'm going to pop upstairs for just a moment. Oh, and look at that sky! That's the bay for you, it can rain at any time. Smells like iodine and seaweed." Sheila could feel the air sag as wind picked up, and thick clouds frowned over the tied-up yachts.

She felt a tug on her sleeve. "I thought you already left," she said as she turned, and looked up into the smiling face of Barry Simmons.

"No, not yet," he said. "At least, not without you." Sheila stood silently.

"I'm sorry to be so forward, but I wanted to meet you. My name is Barry Simmons, 419." His voice was deep, buttered with a southern accent. He held out a large hand; Sheila shook it, keeping her blue eyes on his brown eyes. "And am I correct, you are Mrs. Short, 417?"

Sheila was still silent.

"I'm sorry, have I offended you, ma'am?"

"Forgive me if I seem nonplussed." She paused for a moment, breaking eye contact. "That means—"

"Yes, I know. But that word always makes me feel so insegrevious."

"Um… *insegrevious?*"

"Just a small joke. It's a nonsense word I like to throw around. Word jokes are big with me. Some say I have a hebephrenic sense of humor."

"Hebe…" Sheila looked nonplussed, her eyebrows knitted.

"Having erratic speech and childish mannerisms, that's the most polite definition, ma'am. Please pardon my logorrhea. But—" he spoke to her as he took her elbow and guided her along the front of the building, "but why don't we go somewhere so we can hear each other speak? I wanted to say how much I enjoyed your thoughts at the Board meeting last week." They stepped around the corner to the pergola by the pool.

"My thoughts?! Why, I just told the Board how pleased I am to be here." They sat in side-by-side chaise lounges. The noise from the crowd was barely audible.

"Indeed, ma'am. You were eloquent! A home of one's own—you must be a Virginia Woolf fan too?"

My insteps are melting, Sheila thought, *all the way down to the core of the earth.*

"Well yes, yes, that's right. I am." She paused for a moment. "But please, call me Sheila. Anything, really, except ma'am."

He laughed. "Sorry, that's my overcompensation complex kicking in. I'm a poor boy that made it big—and I do mean big—in the 1970s. I invented a collapsible hair curler.

SofTease. Women could sleep on them without making a hole in their skulls. Have you heard of them?"

"I think so." Sheila reached for her inhaler again, but decided to wait before she used it.

"Made tons of money. Been kicking around ever since. Almost bought this place—" he gestured to the Vinca—"but wanted to wander some more. Spent most of my money, but kept quite a tidy nest egg. Not too profligate, ma'am— *Sheila.*"

Sheila put the inhaler back in her purse, she seemed to be able to breathe easier as the wind continued to build. She started to rise from the lounge.

"And I'm sorry to mix up conversation with autobiography. But I wanted to make a point of speaking to you. Before we get caught up in the bay fracas." He reached out and touched her arm. She felt warm where his flesh touched hers.

"Mr. Simmons, I—"

"Barry, please."

"Very well. *Barry.* I think a bay by any other name is—"

A slap of thunder, a brilliant flash: the storm had arrived. Celeste ran up to them, dangling an empty cocktail glass in one hand and an empty carafe in the other. "Good. Found you. Quickly, both of you, quickly!" She ran back around the corner.

Barry and Sheila followed her into total confusion in the parking lot. The television camerawoman was standing by the building's entrance, and the WSPB-TV reporter was speaking into his microphone. A small crowd was gathered in front of the lobby and standing very still.

Celeste wobbled as she stood beside Sheila. "It was Crooks." With her empty carafe, Celeste gestured to the fourth floor lobby. "Crooks."

"Celeste, sweetie, what do you mean? *What* was Crooks?"

"Oh, that lawyer. He was up on the top floor with the bullhorn, said it looked better, folks could hear better. Flagpole in one hand, bullhorn in the other. Storm started. Then, then..." She looked away from the building, toward the bay.

"What, dear? Then what?"

"Lightning. Got him. Right through the flag pole. Zot." Celeste slumped onto a stone bench in the lobby entrance. "And another thing, probably worse."

Sheila braced herself against Barry. "What, dear? Celeste, what is it? What could be worse?"

"That other lawyer from Tampa, Richards. He was standing right down here, under the flag when, when... when the lightening knocked Crooks over the edge." She twisted her mouth, and said "Splotty-kins. Squished Richards."

Sheila saw Joseph as Celeste leaned into a hedge and made choking sounds. She started to explain to Joseph, but he just shrugged and helped his inebriated wife to their car.

The rain started, a light tattoo, a wet tarantella.

Sheila could hear Arlene Tyler, shouting to other residents that she did not know what was going on. Peg was tooting her scooter horn to clear a path to the parking lot. Clara was smiling at the TV reporter and stepping into the camera's spotlight. Police and medical staff monopolized the elevator, tidying the death at the top and death at the bottom. Yards of yellow tape fluttered everywhere they went.

Sheila and Barry watched the circus of sours. As the tide of onlookers and others began to ebb, Sheila broke the stricken silence. "Do you mind walking me home, Barry?" She fished in her purse for her inhaler. "Long day's journey if ever there was one." They rode up to the fourth floor in silence, and stepped out onto the lobby. The area around the blackened flag pole was draped in bright yellow tape and an acrid odor.

A light breeze slipped by from the bay.

The rain stopped.

The sky cleared.

A rosy glow rubbed the bay and took to the sky. Sheila took a long, deep breath.

"Barry, dear, let's move a little closer to the railing. The view is quite salubrious! Something you can press your cheek up to." Mrs. Sheila Fitzgerald Short, newly of 417 Vinca Terrace, St. Petersburg, Florida, leaned her shoulder against her friend and admired the view of St. Pete Bay.

Veni Vidi Vinca

Vinca Terrace, St. Petersburg, Florida,
April, 1999

Sheila Fitzgerald Short shook her fist at the small plane in morning sky. "Obstreperous fool!" she hissed. The bay breeze tickled her nightgown as she leaned against the railing of the walkway that flanked her condo building. The plane, and the illuminated sign it dragged behind it—Keep Tampa Bay Tampa Bay—banked away from her and bore down on Tampa.

"To an inner circle of hell with you! You wake me up, drag your hideous sign over my home, then fly away. There is no excuse for buzzing around so damn early in the morning!" She coughed hard, pulled her nightgown tighter. "You freak, you fool, you molecule!"

From behind her, she heard a deep voice. "Sheila, honey, please move back from railing. It's windy out here, you'll catch cold, and that wouldn't be too salubrious now, would it? And yelling Cole Porter lyrics at him won't help, either." Barry Simmons put his arm around Sheila's thin frame and guided her into the open door of her condo. Over their shoulders, over the bay, the small plane dragged its sign into the dawn.

"Sorry, sweetie, just raging against the day." Sheila sighed as she dropped into the deep cushions of her rattan sofa. Her long fingernails slid across the cushions, *kwhip, kwhip,* as she searched for her monogrammed, gold-plated inhaler—a gift from Barry. "But the bay, Barry, the bay. And that crazy sign. Keep Tampa Bay Tampa Bay. Gertrude Stein would be proud, proud, proud."

"Gertrude Stein? Don't know her work, but the sign is wrong, wrong, wrong. Right?" Barry called from the open-concept kitchen to the open-concept living room-great room. "Cold press coffee coming right up. Get it while it's cold." He placed a tray with their coffee and Salted Caramel Pot de Crème on the coffee table.

"Is this seat saved?" He sat beside her on the couch, and leaned against her. She placed a delicate hand on his tan, beefy arm.

"Barry, my darling darling," Sheila said, her blue eyes on his brown eyes. "We *must* do something."

He flashed a Hollywood smile at her. "Oh, eager to try out my new Viagra?" He patted his shirt pocket; a foil packet crinkled.

"Please be serious, Barry. The St. Pete Bay issue isn't finished, despite what the coroner said. Those gruesome deaths. I can't help but imagine we will see more legal shenanigans from Matty O'Johns and his cohorts."

"Sheila, Sheila, this is beginning to sound like an episode of *McMillan & Wife*."

Her face was as blank as the bay before dawn. Then she frowned. "I don't get your reference, Barry, but we must eschew cleverness for its own sake." She sipped her coffee, and put a spoon in her dessert.

"Are you on docent duty this morning?" He helped her up then held her for a few moments. "Or can we try my new—"

"Barry, I've been studying for my docent exam for several months. I passed the first two exams, and today is my last one. But after ... well, please don't forget where you put those pills!" Sheila gave him an impish look and headed for her bedroom. "Be right out. Help yourself to some more pot de crème."

"Must dash home," he called to her, "got some legal finagling to do. If you want me, you know where I live! Take a right, two doors down." He closed the front door softly;

Sheila could hear him whistling as he made his way to his own condo.

Finished dressing, Sheila stood in front of the mirror on her bedroom door and adjusted her new fascinator, giving it a jaunty tilt. She turned to look at herself over her shoulder. "Well," she muttered to herself, "as Pope Francis said, 'it's beautiful if you look at it from the front. But if you look at it from behind, you discover the truth.' " She dropped her inhaler into her purse and headed out her door into the brave new world of being a docent.

*   *   *   *   *

Tyrone Square Mall,
Hats Again Kiosk

A mall kiosk, Tiffany Rebecca Ursula Mercedes Palma thought, *is not very safe. Not in an emergency, anyways. Get a gol dang fire going, crowd runs wild through the mall, first thing you know they push over anything in their way. Hats over tea kettle, I guess. Maybe if this flimsy kiosk weren't smack dab in the middle of a hallway.... My intuition tells me something very bad is going to happen, some kind of upside down trouble.*

"Hey, lady, do you really make all these yourself? And what's a fascinator??" A tourist in a hot-pink bathing suit and Hawaiian shirt fondled a fascinator that dangled a Hand Made-Recycled Materials tag. Tiffany saw a trail of cookie crumbs the tourist just deposited on her velvet fascinator; she wrinkled her nose at the bad mix of several perfume samples floating around the sunburned woman. *She's a taker*, Tiffany thought. *I pity those folks at Perfume World, and anyone with a nose in this hemisphere.*

"Yes, yes, I make these myself. They're small hats that clip on to your head. Some folks call them a cocktail hat. I research designs from old Hollywood movies, and—"

"Can I try this on?" asked the tourist, "I like the color." She reached to take the hat off its stand. But Tiffany was faster than the slow-moving woman, and grabbed the feathered-and-sequined hat first.

"Here," she said, "Let me help you with that." The woman leaned forward, Tiffany leaned over the counter, and the woman leaned back wearing a genuine-imitation-recycled-handmade hat before she could blink. Tiffany helped her adjust the veil.

"Oh," said the tourist, pouting in the large mirror standing on the counter, "oh, I thought it was royal blue. Guess it was just the light over it." She reached to take the hat off her head, but Tiffany was faster again. "Got any bathing caps?" The woman took a Nokia cherry-red phone out of her large straw beach bag and began dialing before Tiffany could tell her no, no bathing caps. Tiffany shook her head, and the hatless tourist walked away in a Sears-wise direction.

I woulda thought opening a bookstore in the mall woulda brought in a higher class of folks, guess the food court kinda cancelled that out, thought Tiffany. *Roofing was an easier way to earn a buck. Well, saner, anyway. No tourists. And the mall is quiet today, lots of nothing going on.*

She reached into a drawer below the counter and pulled out a dog-eared copy of a brochure on how to prepare for the Y2K catastrophe, the world's end that would arise in just a few months.

*   *   *   *   *

Lobby of O'Johns and Richards Law Firm
Washington, DC

"Mr. O'Johns, when should I tell callers you'll be back from Florida?" The receptionist from the temp agency asked Matty O'Johns as he rushed by the Reception Desk and jabbed the elevator call button repeatedly.

"Don't!" he barked as he stepped into the elevator and jabbed the button to close the door. He said aloud to the slow-closing door, "Damn fools, what a mess they've made. Hope to hell they didn't leave anything that points to the firm. Getting killed is bad enough, but sloppy work is intolerable." He jabbed the close button again, and punched the button for the Parking Garage.

He found his car and drove out of the parking garage as fast as he could. His car protested his rough handling, but O'Johns pressed on, away, around, not stopping until he was at Baltimore-Washington Airport. Out of his car, into the airport, through security, into his seat: he was an angry blur.

Tampa International Airport did little to satisfy him. His room at the Vinoy Park Hotel did little to satisfy him. He was, however, happy that his hotel overlooked the bay, a short walk from Vinca Terrace, and Albert Whitted Airport.

"Got all my ducks in a row," he said to his empty hotel room. "How's *that* for planning?" He stripped to his shorts, leaned back against the mountain of pillows on his king-sized bed, and sipped aged whiskey as he counted the points of his plan on his stubby fingers. "Keep annoying the city with those anti-Tampa Bay signs, close the Vinca, buy it, tear it down, sell it for an *obscene* profit—my *favorite* kind— and kick out all those pesky old folks. Including that iceberg, Sheila Short. And I even get to bribe someone. Deceit is as good as the truth, especially if you make a profit!" His laugh merged with a burp. He raised his glass in salute to his unpleasant image in the wall mirror.

The room telephone rang, a melodious intrusion into the growing glow of O'Johns' whiskey-fed stupor. He barked hello into the receiver.

A throaty voice said, "Still on for tomorrow at noon, Revenge Café?

"What?!"

"Revenge Café. Noon tomorrow."

"Who IS this?" O'Johns climbed out of the canyon of pillows and sat on the edge of his bed. His boxer shorts gaped. He burped again.

"No need for names, you said. Remember, O'Johns?"

"Oh, oh yeah. Almost asleep there." He scratched the gap. "Noon tomorrow, you make sure you're—"

"And bring the money." Throaty voice hung up.

O'Johns held the receiver until it started to wail. He hung up the phone, shuffled to his balcony window, and looked out at the blinking control tower of the nearby Albert Whitted airfield.

"It's all or nothing," he muttered, and poured himself another drink. "To Vinca and victory. Or as that poor bastard Richards said, do or die. *Quo vadis*, Richards, just *where are you going?* Oh, wait, you can't tell me where you're going. You can't tell anybody nothing." He laughed and burped again, then headed back into his pillow canyon for a troubled night's sleep.

* * * * *

Cold Dishes

O'Johns opened the passenger door of his tax and stepped out into the Florida day. He winced at the bright perpendicular sun that fell straight down on his head, and ran his tongue across his dehydrated lips. "That sun's a killer," he said to the driver as he handed him his fare. "And this IS the Revenge Café, right?"

The taxi driver leaned out his window and said, "Yes and no."

"Listen, smartass—"

"Take it easy buddy. Used to be called Rache Café. Guess no one knew what it meant so they changed it."

O'Johns looked at the sign above the modest stucco building, and could see the old name through the fresh paint of the new name. "Damn city, always changing names." He burped again and slammed the cab door. The driver gunned his cab and left his fare to suck down a cloud of blue exhaust.

He stepped out of the dazzling sun through the revolving door into coolness and darkness, nearly tripping over the welcome mat. "Damn thing, nearly broke my neck!" he sputtered. Once his eyes adjusted, he saw a less-than-dazzling interior: wooden booths with peeling paint, faded lime-green stucco walls with flaking patches, water-damage spots on the ceiling's acoustic tiles, and a floor strewn with peanut shells. In the back right corner was a small stage, just big enough for two wooden bar stools. Nailed through the gray burlap on the walls behind it were cracked glossy black-and-white pictures of Tommy Gumina, and the brothers Guido and Pietro Deiro and their accordions.

A diner-style counter ran the length of the café, and was topped with dark brown Formica®. On the wall behind the counter was a sign that said "Best Served Cold" in shaky letters that made it look like a ransom note. At the far end of the counter, just beside the hallway to the restrooms, sat the only customer: a man in a straw hat, aviator sunglasses, Hawaiian shirt, baggy white shorts, and flip-flops. "You'll know me when you see me," throaty voice had told O'Johns earlier that week, "just look for a tourist." He swiveled on his counter stool when O'Johns stumbled on the entrance mat. He waved O'Johns toward a small booth against a wall.

"So," said throaty voice, "you made it." He was about thirty-five, curly black hair, stubble and bright-blue eyes.

O'Johns sat and used a napkin to brush crushed peanuts off the soles of his shoes. "Let's make this quick. Is the new sign ready, the banner?"

"Try the Gazpacho and Watermelon Feta Salad," said throaty. "Skip the iced tea, too sweet." He turned and waved over a waiter, then opened his wallet and cleaned out old business cards.

O'Johns waived the waiter away. He slid a plain manila envelope toward Throaty.

"Look, I didn't come here for the food or the crazy music. It's all sand in my mouth. Just tell me: is the sign ready?"

Throaty looked out the window and squinted. "Yeah, yeah, it's ready. First thing tomorrow." He turned and looked at O'Johns, deeply, unmistakably, as he picked up the envelope.

"And get one thing right. This is *my* plane, *my* flight, *my* license. All you're getting for your money is a ride in the front seat. Don't know what you're up to and don't care, but it's more than your fool neck at risk here. The rules are clear, no passengers, no flying unapproved banners. Don't know what that crap *Veni vidi vici Vinca* means and I don't care."

He continued, squinting to establish his disapproval. "But one wrong move and you're out on your head. Out, got me, even if we're over the bay."

Before he could reply, O'Johns heard a squawk of feedback from the speakers in the corner. The lights were on over the stage, and a young man sat on a wooden bar stool, tapping the microphone as he unstrapped the bellows of his accordion, stretching its black load over his heart. "Afternoon everyone," he boomed. "Welcome to our tribute to the accordion music of Pietro Deiro, the daddy of the accordion. Remember, please, you are as much a part of the music as an observer is part of the quantum-mechanical equation."

Before the guitarist could join the accordion player on the stage, Matty crunched his way across the shells and out the front door. "Seven o'clock sharp!" he bellowed over his shoulder to Throaty.

*   *   *   *   *

Law Office of Russian Reeves, LLC,
St. Petersburg, Florida

"Mr. Simmons, thank you for coming in to see me. My friends call me Russ, short for Russian, a family name. And yes, you are right, Mr. Simmons, it looks like they've been up to some sneaky transactions." Russ Reeves settled back in his leather chair, and looked across his desk at Barry Simmons. "Very sneaky."

Barry clenched his fist, then released it slowly. He looked back across the desk at the young, blond, lawyer with Hollywood teeth.

Russ tapped a folder on his desk. "It took some doing, but I was able to trace back several dummy corporations to O'Johns and Richards, most of them in a little town in Colorado called Broken Bone. They're poised to buy the Vinca. It also looks like they're planning to raze it and then sell the land to the city. And they may be behind the resistance to renaming the bay, probably to irritate the city. Sounds petty—and it is—but it's been shown to be very effective."

"What bald temerity! I figured it was something like that. Anything we can do to stop them?"

Russ looked out his window at the traffic on 54th Avenue. Shoppers, tourists, and pedestrians marched by on their way in and out of the Eagles Park Shopping Center. His store-front office gave him a panoramic view of both 54th Avenue and Park Street. "Well," he said, and stood up to look out the window. "Two things. One is a big thing. Big for you, especially. The other, well, the other thing would be if *snap*—" he snapped his fingers—"Matty O'Johns disappears. I've been saying "they" but it's all down to him now. Without him, the whole deal would collapse."

"I like the sounds of the second proposition. But the first plan?"

Reeves rubbed the cleft in his chin. "Fire with fire. Meaning we set up dummy corporations, too, and buy the Vinca before O'Johns gets wise. Then, and this is an important part, give the Vinca to all the owners as a gift. It can be done tax free, too!"

Barry Simmons blinked hard, then laughed. "But where, or who, or—well, where would the purchase money come from? Who is the sugar daddy in this deal?"

Russ leaned forward across the desk, gave Barry a big dimpled smile, and said, "I'm looking at one sweet sugar daddy right now." He leaned back and tented his fingers.

"Well," he blinked again, "well. That would be salubrious, wouldn't it? Not to mention take care of holiday gifts for the rest of my life." He stood up, looked out Russ's windows, stretched, and turned back to his lawyer. "Can I afford this without beggaring myself?" His eyebrows—gull wings— pushed up his forehead, his forehead pushed back his hairline, and Barry felt a knot growing at the base of his neck.

"Yes and no. No, as it stands right now. But yes, if... if you sell your rights to *SofTease*."

Barry sat down. He added a few moments of silence to eternity, then looked at Russ. "Would anyone else know? Could anyone else figure it out? And listen to us, we sound as conspiratorial as O'Johns!"

Through his perfect dentition, Russ said, "Unrecorded history, unhappening as it unfolds. No one should know, no one could know, no one. They," he pointed over his shoulder to the diplomas on his wall, each from a top-notch law school and university, "guarantee it." He opened his desk drawer and pulled out another folder of papers. "These are in case you said yes. I was an Eagle scout, and you know our motto." He aimed a long finger at another framed certificate above the leather sofa beside his desk. "Ready?"

*   *   *   *   *

Albert Whitted Airport,
St. Petersburg, Florida

"So you're telling me we pick up the sign *after* we take off?" O'Johns was standing just inches from Throaty—close enough to see the name tag Andrew Higgins stenciled on his flight suit—as the sky grew lighter over the bay. He had Higgins pinned against the DHC-1 Chipmunk. Even in the dim light, the airplane was a brilliant yellow. The name *Sky Turtle* was hand painted in shaky, dark red letters. A clear acrylic canopy, strong as steel, was the only way in, or out, of the confining cockpit: it was an oubliette, its only exit was up.

"We fly through those damned goal posts over there and snatch the damned banner?!"

Higgins turned in the few inches between them and climbed into the rear seat of the airplane. "Yes. Get in. We don't have much time." He nodded east cross the bay, toward Tampa. "When the sun is full up it makes taking off over water very tricky." O'Johns stood still.

"Okay," said Higgins as he started to slide the canopy closed, "then you don't get in. I'll leave you."

O'Johns stopped the canopy with his hand and climbed into the front seat of the plane. Higgins slid the bubble closed. He tapped O'Johns on the shoulder and pointed to the safety harness. "Buckle up or the engine won't start. And put on your headset," he said loudly into his passenger's ear. Before O'Johns could respond, Higgins started the engine.

As they taxied down the runway, Higgins said into his microphone, "We take off, then circle back and pick up the banner. Great view up front, right?" He could imagine a swarm of doubts around O'John's head as the earth said goodbye to the flying machine.

Up, around, the plane drilled into the St. Petersburg air, its grapple hook and towline tucked in like a papoose. Higgins took a tight turn around the airstrip, and brought his aircraft just a few feet off the ground to link his hook to the banner: low and slow. O'Johns groaned and sputtered filth into his microphone.

A batsman, standing to the side of the banner, signaled Higgins to start a steep climb, full power. "Hang on. We should get a slight jolt that means we got the banner, and a confirmation signal. Any second now." The pilot could see only the back of his passenger's head, a head that blocked the confirmation wave from the batsman. The *Air Turtle* bounced in an updraft from the bay. "Any ... second ... now..."

"Where the hell is it?" O'Johns hissed into his headset. "You fool, you missed it!"

Higgins growled. Could his belligerent passenger be right? Did they catch the banner?

"Turn back, turn back NOW and get that damned sign!!" O'Johns' bellows did not need a microphone. "Now, or the deal's off, damn you..."

Higgins growled again. "Didn't see the confirmation wave. Don't always feel the jolt. Foolish to turn back." *Your weight,* Higgins thought, *is throwing me off. If I could just slide this bubble open real quick... no, we're not high enough yet to be sure it would kill him....*

"Do it or you're dead." O'Johns unbuckled, and started to turn as much as he could in the confined space.

Higgins sighed. "Easy, bucko. Going back," he said feebly into the microphone. O'Johns buckled up again.

Higgins started a turn, then saw his air speed drop: The banner WAS attached! He yelled "Hang on," and fought to bring the plane out of a spiral as the banner—flaccid, heavy—tugged them down. The engine stalled.

Another updraft from the bay caught the plane to pull it to the sky, but the banner resisted and pulled the plane down, just a few feet from the ground. Too low, too slow to resist the tug of war—the plane flipped. A flightless bird, the *Sea Turtle* slipped down to earth and landed on its canopy.

Blood rushed to Higgins' head, his arms fell useless upward to the top of the canopy. The side of his head knocked against the plexiglass, leaving a small, bright red smear and a small, dark moment of unconsciousness. "What... ?" His eyes fluttered for a few moments.

The *Sky Turtle* rocked lightly in the wind, an upturned palm. The banner, *Vini Vidi Vici Vinca,* stretched across the runway perfectly flat, as if ironed.

Higgins shook his head to clear his mind. The rising sun's red halo appeared around his passenger's silhouette; O'Johns stirred. As Higgins leaned forward to tap him on the shoulder, he heard the wail of the airfield's rescue truck through the pounding in his ears.

O'Johns muttered "Get me out of this damned thing."

"Help will be here any second, just wait," Higgins rasped.

"Hello, no, I can't get caught here. No way am I—"

"—No, NO. Do NOT unbuckle, just wait—"

"—going to stay." Higgins heard a sharp *snick* as O'Johns released his safety harness, then a sickening *crack* as Matty O'Johns fell straight down, toward the canopy.

And broke his neck.

*   *   *   *   *

Tyrone Square Mall, Hats Again Kiosk
One week later

Tiffany reached across the counter of her kiosk and gave the fascinator on her customer's head a jaunty tilt. "There, *that* should do it! You look wonderful."

"This is marvelous. I am impressed that you make all these yourself!" The very thin woman blinked through dense glasses at her image in the mirror on the corner of the counter. "Quite insouciant, don't you think, Celeste?"

"Yes, dear, I think so too. Quite festive. What is it made of, dear?"

Tiffany leaned toward the women, more out of concern for any hearing deficiencies than a need to share a secret. "Remember that plane that crashed last week? Over at Whitted Airport? Well, my uncle helped tow it away, horrible mess. Miracle it didn't slide into the bay." *Hmmm*, Tiffany wondered, *could* that *be what my intuition was trying to tell me?*

She took a sip of her Dr Pepper and continued. "Anyway, he cut off some of the bright yellow fabric from the wing and even a chunk of that nice acrylic stuff on top. See those clear squares? I chopped up the clear stuff and glue-gunned them on to the yellow. Hate to see good material go to waste. Seize the day, I always say. Cool, right?"

"Yes, I *do* remember the day quite clearly, it was a red letter day indeed." Sheila removed her hat and handed it back to Tiffany. "So please wrap it up! It will be a memento of the good news I got that day. Everyone at Vinca got good news that day."

"Oh, Sheila, don't you think it's a bit maudlin, too? I mean, that poor man *died*. Lucky thing the pilot wasn't hurt."

"Oh, I don't know," Sheila said as she handed Tiffany payment for her fascinator. Her eyes sparkled like pieces of broken acrylic on her new hat. *"Vita brevis*, don't you know? And, as my darling Barry says, *veni vidi Vinca!"*

Vinca Terrace, St. Petersburg, Florida,
May, 2009

"I think you'll like this, Celeste. If I can find it on the map." Sheila Fitzgerald Short stood with her back to the periwinkle columns of her condo home, Vinca Terrace. She faced the bay, its late spring breeze an antidote to the intense Florida sun. Sun, land, and sky warred for her attention. Beside her, Celeste Lobosco, her life-long friend, fidgeted with the Majorica pearls clutching her neck.

A jogger passed them by; she was dressed in a bright yellow baseball cap, headphones, a surgical mask, a bright yellow halter top with matching shorts, elastic knee braces, and bright yellow jogging shoes. Her skin glistened with a thick layer of sun block. She jinked, as if she were pulling a heavy weight along the walkway beside Bayshore Drive.

Sheila snapped open her map of St. Petersburg, Florida, and said to Celeste, "Albert Whitted Park. I've heard it's a very nice place, with a grand view of the water. I'm certain it will be the perfect place to say goodbye to Angie!" She pushed her prescription glasses against the bridge of her nose, concentrated on the map, and placed a bone-thin hand on Celeste's arm. "Please help me find the park on this map, I can't see the details here. I believe our destination might be under the G."

"Under the G? That sounds mysterious." Celeste Lobosco squinted at her friend as she stood in the evaporating shade of the condo building. The sun swung from the bay into downtown St. Petersburg. Celeste's blue cotton skirt and loose yellow blouse were flapping flags; her carefully hennaed hair misbehaved.

"Yes, of course. Look at the map. We're about here." She speared a pale pink fingernail at their spot on her map and dragged it across the peninsula. "See how the words *St. Petersburg* stretch from the Gulf to the bay? Our destination is trapped just under the G, I imagine. And besides which, this map is riddled with strange symbols."

Celeste's eyebrows quirked. "Zounds. I would have thought it would have a legend."

"Yes. Yes, it does. But," Sheila tipped her head forward, making her sunglasses slip, "legends aren't always facts. Maps seem to have limits. If I had a map that could tell me who I would have been if I had stayed in any of the places I have lived and left, well... I guess *that* would be quite a legend."

Celeste took the map from Sheila and studied it for a few moments. She folded it, and put it in the palm leaf beach bag she used as a purse. She took Sheila's thin elbow and turned her to face the north, toward the Vinoy. "Here, I believe this will help, for starters. Now you are facing in the same direction as the map."

"Celeste, I find this whole waterside, this *waterfront*, such a pinking shears jumble. There is simply *nothing* that *looks* like Albert Whitted Park on that map. Besides which," she said, and pushed wisps of her complicated chignon back under her straw hat, "didn't you once tell me that St. Petersburg is a grid? A grid sounds salubrious. I much prefer a simple geometry."

More elaborate hand gestures let Celeste know her friend was agitated, in turmoil. "You know I like the familiar, I like home."

"Ye gods and gadzooks, Sheila. And tutty-kins, too. I know you don't go out much, but it's been years since you moved here. Yes?"

"Yes, I admit it freely. I'm like a sailboat listening to the wind, a wind that keeps saying, 'Back to the shore, quick, quick!" She took an audible breath, and continued. "And yet I want to sail close to the wind sometimes. Anyway, I digress. A man told me the park is 'a peninsula on a peninsula on a peninsula'. But nothing on the map looked anything like that," Sheila sniffed. "He must be a Gertrude Stein fan."

Celeste said to the bay breeze, "Sounds like this man told you a lot of things."

Sheila continued. "Well, maybe he was right. Florida is a peninsula, St. Petersburg is a peninsula, and the park is on a peninsula. Though I would think it's more like headlands." Sheila illustrated her point with wide gestures that made her puka shell bracelet dance.

"Yes, sweetie, I'm certain it is. I believe it will take us about half an hour to walk there. And," she linked elbows with Sheila, "the bonus is that we get to see them working on the new Salvador Dalí Museum. If I read the map correctly, the park is directly opposite the new museum. Under the G, as you say. My husband says it looks like an above-ground bomb shelter, but Joseph is not too keen on modern art."

"Yes, the same man I spoke to about the park said the museum 'has a certain syrup but it doesn't pour.' I'm convinced he is a convicted Gertrude Stein fan. So, shall we split, just as if we were infinitives? Off to the headlands!"

They waved goodbye to the Vinca, crossed Bayshore Drive, and headed along the serpentine sidewalk southwise. It was a perfect afternoon in St. Petersburg, cuddled up against the bay. Sheila and Celeste were in the glorious teatime of their life. Palm tree pom-poms rustled to cheer them on, the clear sky was a perfect fascinator, a day moon grinned. The sun rehearsed for its hot summer.

"Joseph recommends that we stop on our way back and have lunch at a darling little restaurant, *Alfresco's*. It's right here, right at the foot of the pier, and practically at your doorstep. Their outdoor deck is elegant and cool even in this weather." She pointed to the small bistro wedged across Bayshore Drive and the road to the pier. A small statue of Christopher Columbus stood at the entrance to the pier, arms crossed, watching over native Floridians and tourists alike.

"Yes, I feel a bit peckish. And that boîte looks the perfect place to escape this salty heat."

"Perhaps we can spot some of those famous green parakeets. How could Charles Darwin ever call them a pest?"

Slow, loose-armed, and breeze-cooled, the two friends walked to find their place under the G.

*　*　*　*　*

"Lawks-a-mussy, is this *leviathan* the new Dalí Museum? Will this frog become a prince? All this tortuosity, it's a cement vault. Humph. Intellectually frowzy. Meretricious." Sheila stood, arms akimbo, looking at the museum under construction. She pushed her straw hat off her head, its thin string holding it along the back of her blue-and-white seersucker pantsuit.

"Yes, yes, it does look as if someone played Mad Libs with the architect's plans." Celeste took the map out from her tote and held it up to block the view of the unfinished building.

"I have an angry sense of doubt about this building, Celeste. I do miss giving tours at the so-called old museum, but I'm not certain I would feel comfortable working in this, this, ... calaboose!"

"Now, Sheila. Do you really mean that? If nothing else, Joseph tells me it will be able to withstand a Category 5 hurricane, and it's well above flood level!"

"Fanning with damp praise, I suppose." Sheila retrieved a shiny gold inhaler from her shell-shaped pocket book, took a puff, stood fully upright, and turned her back on the construction and upturned earth. "I believe Albert Whitted Park is straight ahead."

"Ye gods and gadzooks! Joseph and I have been to the Mahaffey Theater many times. But we never *noticed* this small park nearby, right beside Albert Whitted airport. So many things to see right here, as you said, under the G. And is that a *playground* I see at the end of the park?"

"You have the eyes of an eagle. Barry said yes, they put in a playground a few years ago. All the playthings are shaped like airplanes. Very clever, what with its proximity to the airport. I don't doubt it will inspire a whole new generation of Amelia Earharts and Charles Lindberghs, and perhaps even another Pancho Barnes. Shall we reconnoiter?"

"Yes, this looks like the perfect place to remember Angie." At the mention of their friend's name, both women drooped. Across the bay, a sewage plant burped gray clouds from its tall smoke stacks. Floating in the water nearby, a patch of dead vegetation and bay trash trapped a seagull. The bird bobbed and cried as it tried to free its feet. The rotting stink made itself available to anyone at hand.

*   *   *   *   *

Lunch Alfresco

"Glory-kins, Sheila. Isn't this as charming as Joseph said it would be?"

Sheila looked up, gave a quick smile, and flipped the menu over again.

"Oh. I know that look. That smile. What's wrong, sweetie?" Celeste reached across the small table and rested her fingertips lightly on her friend's arm. As she drew her arm back, her bracelet snagged on one of the seashells embedded in the polyurethane that decorated the tabletop.

"Certainly it can't be the view." She nodded at the bay that wrapped itself around the restaurant's deck; it was chock-a-block with berthed pleasure craft, their masts scratching a toothy skyline. Behind the boats, between palm trees, the quiet airport tower watched land and water, and the sky that covered them.

Their table, snugged up against the railing, was a few feet away from a signpost nailed to a loblolly piling atilt the water. Faded painted letters gave the distance to Singapore, L.A., Penetanguishene, Stamford, and other ports.

"And I know you're not a fan of baseball, or what you call sports games, but we could practically spit—expectorate, as you would say—into Al Lang Stadium from here. Joseph and I enjoy their occasional amateur and exhibition baseball games. It's right over there, you can see their tall lights." Celeste pointed over Sheila's shoulder. "No matter where you sit, you have a wonderful view of the harbor and the bay, just in case."

"In case?" Sheila tilted her face.

"Yes. In case you were to actually go there and were unendingly bored by the game!"

They shared girlish giggles.

The wooden planks beneath their feet bounced in rhythm as staff and other diners passed their table. Singapore, Penetanguishene, L.A., and Stamford kept their distance as they enjoyed their lunch. The restaurant's syrupy music from the 1980s was as insidious as the breeze.

During a lapse in the music, Celeste asked "Sheila, what's that hum? That low frequency. Do you hear it too? Definitely not part of the music."

Sheila cocked an ear. "Oh, why yes, I do hear a curious susurration. It sounds like one of those binaural beats Dickie was telling me about. But more distinct, if we can hear it without headphones. And it seems to be growing louder."

Celeste half rose from her seat. "Ah, there it is! Over there, sweetie, over your shoulder, over the bay. By the airfield tower, do you see that bright yellow plane?"

A large plane banked around the airport's tower.

"Yes, yes, I do see it. And what a coincidence. I was just re-reading the passage in *Mrs. Dalloway* where a plane flies overhead, skywriting a message in smoke signals no one can agree on. Very symbolic. And quite advanced."

"Yes, well... here's another coincidence. Do you see that the plane just flew near the ground and picked up a banner?" The yellow plane jinked and strained to pull its heavy weight, a large sign that touted the merits of ... something they could not read with their age-diminished eyesight.

"Perilous, simply perilous. You will *never* catch me riding in such a small craft, much less a *commercial* aircraft!" Sheila turned around to the table, picked at her grouper nuggets, and sighed. "But I still maintain if we could have persuaded Angie to fly, she would have joined us here, and ..."

"Might still be with us?" Celeste offered, returning to her ceviche.

Sheila did not answer for a few moments. "Yes. We could have used a map with the legend that told us she would just let go of life. Our wounded bird. Now... now she's under the G." They both sighed.

They finished their lunch in thoughtful silence, then rose to go.

"Oh, Celeste," Sheila said as she took a last look over the railing, "I have yet to see any of those ephemeral green parakeets you told me about. I had hopes they would join me for morning coffee in Straub Park, perhaps eating seeds from one of those enormous banyan trees, flying among the upper branches, among the vines. And I've seen such strange things in the park's trees that I hope are intended to be artwork."

"The last I saw of the parakeets, they were clustered at a substation in Seminole, making a very loud noise."

Sheila looked blank. Celeste answered over her shoulder as they exited the restaurant. "Sorry, Sheila, a substation— so Joseph tells me—modifies voltage. It changes the current from—"

"No, no. I'm perplexed by Seminole. Seminole? Where is that?"

Celeste stopped suddenly, locking her left foot and cocking her right foot at an angle.

"Oh. Oh, well. I suppose it's north of here, near the Gulf of Mexico. But Sheila... well, never mind, sweetie. But here's that statue of Columbus. Do you mind if I take a picture of you standing by him? Don't ask me why, I just like seeing the two of you together." As Sheila walked to the statue, Celeste muttered, "Just a cautionary memento, I suppose. Or, as Joseph would say, reverse psychiatry."

After she took Sheila's picture, Celeste took her friend's elbow, and pointed her diagonally across the intersection. "And there, of course, is your beloved Vinca. Toad Hall, Joseph calls it. Do you think this is how the astronauts felt when they first looked at the earth from space?"

"Please stop digging. You have, as they say, struck oil. You know—"

"But Sheila, I was only—"

"Yes, dear. I'm not offended. But I'm well aware that I am 'geographically challenged,' as my son tells me." She adjusted her straw hat, and patted her hair. "And I always tell him that it's a sign of intelligence!"

They dawdled back to the Vinca, and sat in its open-air lobby. Celeste called her husband in her cell phone, and he told her he was on his way. As they sat waiting for Joseph, Sheila leaned against her friend and said in a low, confidential voice, "I worry sometimes that I'm becoming more like Angie, withdrawing from the world."

Before Celeste could answer, her husband drove up and sounded the car horn.

"And one more question, Celeste. About the Gulf of Mexico. I imagine you mean the water on the western shore of St. Petersburg. Yes?"

"Yes, of course. Why do you ask?" Celeste opened the passenger door, slid in, and waited for Sheila's answer before closing the door.

"Well, my dear, I cannot fathom why they would name it the Gulf of *Mexico* when it so obviously should be the Gulf of *Florida*. Yes? Remember our rally to rename St. Pete Bay? Not to be jingoistic, though that is very popular these days, but I thought perhaps we could change it to—"

"Joseph, darling-kins, drive home at a mad pace, please, before she renames US!"

*   *   *   *   *

Vinca Terrace,
Two weeks earlier, 3:00 a.m.

Sheila Short stepped across the threshold from her condo's living room onto her balcony. Both rooms were almost, but not quite, totally dark. She moved by touch, her frail hand tracing along the living room walls, feeling the edge of the sliding glass doors, and coming to rest on the curved rattan of her favorite seat. She lowered her spare frame into the oversized saucer chair as though its cushions had nails, and gathered her Crepe de Chine robe.

Through the screens, she could see a few lonely lights from the high-rise buildings along Beach Drive. Any stars in the darkness were hidden in the banks of humid clouds, like beautiful women who were resting in another room.

"Not too many others awake at this hour. The hour of the wolf," she said aloud, to herself, to the world on the ground below her balcony. Then her shoulders trembled, her chest heaved, her eyes burned, and Sheila Short cried in the dark. Inconsolable, pointless, salty, inelegant tears.

"Why," she asked no one. "Why does it hurt me so to lose this friend? I'll never be able to prove that law firm, that evil lawyer, brought about her death." She wiped her tears with the large, loose sleeves of her robe. "And," she sniffed as she spoke to herself, "at my age, I've known so many who have died. I am getting quite maudlin in my advanced years!"

She smoothed her robe and sat upright. "No, I'm quite sure I haven't been this melancholy since... since Dickie's friend went missing, all those years ago." She sighed and stood. "Ah, yes, all those years ago..." and she sat down again.

"How can I remember that ... and how can I forget it? My memories rise then sink without a ripple. Hello and goodbye my husband Jameson, my sweet sister Terry, my father, our beloved neighbor Maggie Thistle ..." Her voice broke.

She rose and headed into her kitchen. "Some fine almond sunset tea should set me to rights, and help me get back to sleep."

But on the way to her kitchen, she was seized with ... she didn't know what to call it, the words for her feelings were not in her vocabulary, not a single verb in her life's dictionary of thought-out actions. As much as she could be said to run, Sheila ran to her front door, flung it open, unlatched the storm door, and threw herself against the railing in front of her condo.

"Damn you, whoever, whatever you are, damn you! How COULD you do this? How could you take her?" She swore. She blasphemed. She struck at the universe with her hoarse voice, a voice that barely crossed the parking lot to the tops of the palm trees in front of the Vinca, sinking before they got to the bay—taking her heart with them.

Comfort and kindness, given and received, crunched in her teeth. "The deal is off, life. You too, death! I get it now." Her voice was only a whisper now, her thin body a toy in the wind. But she kept it up. In the moonlight, under a humid sky, the old woman ranted demands and accusations as she balled her fist against a cruel universe.

Her words left her, her beloved words, and she pushed guttural sounds over the railing, up to crash the clouds. As if to comply, to show they gathered her words, clouds covered the moon.

From out of the shadows, a man stepped up to Sheila: it was Barry Simmons. "Darlin', come home." The soft, deep voice floated over Sheila, each word with sweet round corners. "Let me take you home. The government makes it illegal for its soldiers to hurt themselves. I can't let you suffer any more, can't listen to your scree, at least not tonight." Barry Simmons gingerly scooped up his neighbor, his love, in his still-strong arms and carried her home, familiar and comforting home, home to rest.

*   *   *   *   *

Albert Whitted Park,
Three Weeks Later

"Oh, keep your eyes on your balloons! Hold the ribbons tightly. The breeze is very strong today, and we wouldn't want to lose a balloon. Even the bay seems choppy." Sheila held her hat with one hand, and the white ribbon of her balloon with the other. The sky contradicted the wind and water; it was blue equanimity. "Maybe we should have gone a bit lighter on the helium."

Under the pavilion, gathered around the pair of picnic tables, Angie Spark's friends gathered to say goodbye. A dozen pairs of sad eyes, sliding off each face, came to rest on the early morning bay. The airport tower, at the far end of the park, pointed up without leaving a mark on the new sky.

Sheila stood. "I'm sure Angie would be glad to see you all here. She was very private, very shy, but still... she would be happy to see that we're all still thinking of her. Barry said any room was bigger with her in it." A slow moving finger of air ruffled her coral peplum blouse. Sheila smoothed wrinkles from her white linen Capri pants and sat down.

"But..." Sheila looked toward the airfield, and raised her palm as if to say hello to someone across a street, "but we all know how extra sad this is. All those years she spent, recoiling from the evil she worked with so closely. To trace the cause of Angie's death is to peek at Schrödinger's cat."

Tiffany Palma looked up at the mention of cat. Her face was covered with a black veil attached to a black pillbox hat she made for the occasion; thin strips of a plastic water jug were teased up to look like a feather. Her dark crimson lips parted as if to speak, to interrupt, then closed.

Sheila continued, her voice a soft flute solo. "Perfidy, I say it's a case of perfidy. Perfidy unpunished. Though punishment, like rewards, descends on us unevenly." She looked ahead, toward the bay just beyond where the airfield's tower stood, and a day moon hung a slim grin over Tampa. "At least so far."

Celeste looked across the wooden table, her face a question, as if to ask if Sheila would expound.

"But I grow maudlin. I told you this would be short and sweet. Are we all ready to let go?" In answer, balloons bobbed toward the ceiling of the pavilion, then were reeled in on their white ribbons.

Peg eased her electric scooter to the water's edge, and waved the others to stand beside her. She double-tooted the horn of her electric scooter, gave the air a punch, and said, "You go, girl."

Arlene Tyler boomed out, "Did you say let 'em go? Don't forget to detach your ribbons before you let 'em go. Can't have any of them birds chokin' on the dang things."

Clara Davies waved her balloon in the air, her shoulder making a stiff semi-circle farewell in the space above her head.

Then a dozen star-shaped balloons, like white corpuscles in a blue blood stream, clustered together for comfort, slid from under the G into the sky. On, up, around, the balloons sailed and spiraled through St. Petersburg's skies. The biodegradable gestures made their way up and out of their oubliette. As seen from the bay, nothing special happened— the same nothing special the world shows when tragedy and love rub and tickle us but the world can't be bothered. But in the hearts of her friends, the world spun on a better axis.

Yes and No

Denver International Airport, Colorado,
Late May, 2014

Richard Short leaned against the *Short Airways* counter, watching for his passenger, and knew she should be easy to spot. He hoped his mother remembered the directions he gave her on the phone last night. "After you get off your flight from Tampa, go to the ground floor and look for the *Soaring Society of Boulder* booth. My stand is right beside it. Love you, Mom." Thinking of his phone, he stepped behind the counter to search for it among the cluttered shelves and drawers. Chilly air from a revolving door nearby made a pig's breakfast of his flyers.

"Dickie, darling, move out of that draft, young man. You'll catch a cold, and that wouldn't be too salubrious now, would it?" He didn't need to look up to see who was speaking in that choppy, wispy voice: It was his mother.

"Mom, you're looking wonderful," he said, circling the counter then circling her with a gentle hug and a lie. "Florida seems to agree with you. How was your flight?"

"You are still my favorite sycophant, Dickie. The flight was jejune. Now, where's your colleague, the one who likes to go missing?" Sheila Short leaned against the counter, used an inhaler from her purse, then stood straight again. She smoothed her pant suit with a fine-boned hand.

"I'll explain everything on the way, Mom. It's a short flight home. How's school?"

"The *university* is doing well, thank you. Do we need to stroll far? This airfield is a maze of amazement."

"We can board right here." Richard nodded to the door directly behind *Short Airway*'s counter. "Ready to see the best gift a mother ever gave her son?" He turned his mother to look out the window at a small propeller airplane. Its wings were outstretched arms, its propeller a thin-lipped smile. "There she is! The *Flying Fitz,* that Cessna 152. Beautiful, yes?"

Sheila squinted against the bright sun. "Yes, dear, it's quite elegant."

"All thanks to you, Mom!"

"But give some comfort to my poor comprehension, Dickie. What is a Fitz?"

"I wanted to name it in your honor, but there wasn't enough room on the door to paint The Flying Sheila Fitzgerald Short. But the full name IS painted across the bottom. Just my way to say thanks, Mom!"

"Too much gratitude is unbecoming, young man. Besides," she said as she smoothed her pant suit again, "it was your uncles' money, their *guilt* money, that bought your air machine. Leaving the money to you was the least they could do, after the truth came out about your father." She looked away and said, mostly to herself, "I think someone said let no man's happiness depend on the death of aunts."

"Yes, Mom." Richard put his arm around her waist, pulled her close for a moment, then picked up her small travel bag. They took small steps toward the door but she stopped him just before the exit.

"Just promise me one thing, Dickie, before we get in that mechanism." Sheila looked up at her son through thick prescription sunglasses. "No selfish portraits."

"*Selfish portraits?* What do you mean—"

Sheila wagged her hand; her plastic wristbands juddered. "Oh, I believe they're called something else. *Self portraits,* perhaps?" She wrinkled her nose.

"Mom, I still don't know— Oh, wait. Oh no, oh no: Do you mean *selfies?*" Richard laughed; Sheila stood silently.

"Don't *scoff*, young man. Just a few weeks ago a small aircraft met its end not too far from here. Near Denver, the *Tampa Bay Times* said. Federal officials found self-portraits—their words Dickie—at the crash site and believe it was the cause." Sheila took another puff from her inhaler.

"Sorry, Mom."

She stood to her full height, pushed her dark sunglasses against the bridge of her nose, and nodded toward the airport door. "Excelsior!"

*   *   *   *   *

Homes Again Inc.,
Downtown Broken Bone, Colorado

Eloise Tristler reached across her desk to answer the telephone. She squinted at her computer screen, the mountain of paperwork on her crowded desk hiding the Rockies out her office window. "Homes Again, how may I help you?" she asked the caller and scrunched her eyebrows, annoyed at breaking her progress in billing. She looked at the caller ID and winced; new wrinkles appeared in the soft brown flesh around her eyes.

"Hello, this is Randa D'Arcangelo calling. Is this Eloise?" Not waiting for a response, the caller continued, "I saw the most wonderful kitchen on the Decorating Channel. I've changed my mind about the backsplash I ordered. You know: those glass subway tiles I liked so much last week?"

"Um... yes, Mrs. D'Arcangelo. I remember. What, what... what would you like instead?" Eloise cradled the phone under her chin and forced a few commands into her computer keyboard.

"I think the antique tin tiles I just saw would strike just the right note. Is that a problem?"

A moment passed before Eloise answered. "Well. I mean, Mrs. D'Arcangelo. I see that we've *already ordered* your glass tiles, there would be a charge to—"

"Oh, no problem, Eloise. No problem. And I've been thinking about the marble for the downstairs bathroom vanity. I'm not sure if the marble has enough *movement*, do you see? The Realty Twins always use marble with a lot of *movement*." Eloise pictured the movement of a head striking a marble vanity. She took a deep breath and waited just long enough to convey her disapproval.

"Mrs. D'Arcangelo? Here's the thing—"

"Yes, Eloise?

"Our quarry man would be seven kinds of upset if we changed your order *again*." But her remark went unheard over the noise of sawing and hammering on the other end of the line. "Mrs. D'Arcangelo? Can you hear me? Mrs. D'Arcangelo??"

"Eloise, dear, thanks too much. I must call you later. It's demo day and I have to keep a sharp eye on the crew doing the reno on my bonus room. Ta, ta!"

With deliberate movements, Eloise pressed the phone's disconnect button and placed it in the charger. "Why," she asked the air, "does just talking to her make me feel like I dropped my wallet in the toilet?" *And*, Eloise thought but didn't want to say aloud, *doesn't she realize that someday I'll be* mayor *of this whole crazy place, and first thing I'll do is* cancel *some building permits?!*

She pushed out of her creaky wooden office chair, its rusty wheels registering pain, and walked around her shabby desk to stand in front of the poster beside the entrance. Yes and No, it said in large letters. Below the words was a picture of a twisted belt, and below the picture the words "Have a Day."

"Yes," she said again to the air, "I'll be mayor. Won't *they* have a day with that?!" Dimples collected on her soft toffee cheeks. "Won't they *just* have a day!"

*   *   *   *   *

Broken Bone Junior High School

"Can anyone tell me what *anacrusis* means? You know, that thing I do every time we get ready to start playing?" Silence. Kevin D'Arcangelo stood up from his conductor's chair and looked at his junior high school band. He waved his baton in an upward arc, and asked "Does this give you a clue?"

A flute player in the front row raised her hand, and said in a tentative voice, "A preparation beat?"

"Well I'll be a dog and a cat, that's it, that's it exactly, Gwen. Exactly!" He sat back down, all smiles, all teeth, looking at each of his young musicians. "Whether it's music or life, be ready, ladies and gentlemen, be ready! Otherwise, why show up? Preparation is everything. Graduation is at eight o'clock sharp, so take your places in the auditorium by 7:30 tonight. When I give the *anacrusis*, I want to see you all ready. Next year most of you graduate, so let's play our best."

The room in front of him was arranged in semicircular tiers. Flutes, clarinets, and one lonely oboe sat on the first tier, on the second tier were trumpets, trombones, and saxophones, and the top tier was home to a bombastic percussion section.

The band leader swung his baton up and waited for all eyes to meet his; on his downbeat, twenty-three aspiring musicians lay into the inner workings of *Pomp and Circumstance*.

Nearly all the band members finished at the same time. Kevin rapped the conductor's stand for attention. "Well done!

Remember to warm up in the band room *before* you report to the auditorium. Dismissed!"

Trumpets, saxophones, and clarinets disappeared into their cases. Over the adolescent hubbub, Kevin yelled "And don't forget to *bring your music!*" to the backs of the students still within earshot. He gave an absent-minded tug on his graying beard, and looked out over the empty chairs. "Not with a whimper or a bang, but with a tired old tune," he said to himself. "It's been a good run, more than I expected. Or even prepared for."

He took careful steps off the conductor's platform to favor his knees and hold up his sagging pants. *Am I getting too careful,* he wondered, *is that what growing older is all about?* As he straightened the music stands, he hummed to himself. A rhythmic knock made him turn as the band room door swung open.

"Well, Professor Hill, ready to send your last batch into the world?" Aria O'Malley hung in the doorway, a bright-headed moon in the dark entrance. She came in and sat down in the empty oboe player's chair.

Kevin put his thumbs under imaginary suspenders, and said, "Yes, Miss Paroo. They are all graduates of the Think System." He walked to the back of the room, taking the raised steps gingerly, and snugged covers over the kettle drums. As he pulled heavy drapes across the tall windows, hiding the view of Lake No One, he asked "So, Mademoiselle Math Teacher, how go your math wizards? Ready for vacation?"

"Oh, they'll probably spend their summers solving equations around the camp fire. And speaking of fire… " She stood and mimed smoking a cigarette. "Want to tag along while I break the law? Remember: school's out! Not to mention this is your very last day."

He hesitated. "You're a bad influence, I'm glad to say. Just don't tell Randa. My wife thinks smoking is contagious." He headed for the exit and turned out the lights. *Just hope these kids are ready for what life will bring them*, he thought, *or I was as useful as a tuba in a typhoon.*

Aria linked arms with him, smiled, and walked him out the door. He threw the deadbolt and started down the hall toward the front of Broken Bone Junior High, but Aria gently tugged him in the other direction. Outside, he followed her around the bulge of the band room, through the ankle-high scruffy grass that grew behind the school.

"Where are you taking me?"

"Oh, a little place I found recently." At the corner, Aria stopped to take a cigarette and lighter out of her handbag.

Kevin said "Man, you can't smoke at school!"

"I'm not. *Man.* But I'm *ready* to smoke anywhere, any time."

"Oh, your own private anacrusis." She looked puzzled, small twists in her young and unmapped face. Twenty-eight is an awful age.

"Anacrusis," he said, "you know, a musical term. It means a preparation beat. Like when a drummer bangs his drumsticks to count in the band."

She shrugged. "Look." She pointed to the ladder that stretched up to the roof.

"Are you *kidding?* Maybe you can climb that, but I'm at least *twice* your age. That roof's got to be thirty feet up, or more. And my knees …"

Aria tucked the cigarette behind her ear and put the lighter in her pants pocket. She slung her handbag over her shoulder. "Not afraid of heights, are you?" she teased, one hand on the ladder.

"No. No. At least I never used to be. Used to love being up high." He waited for her to clear a few rungs, hiked up his sagging pants, then followed her. "I'm on your six," he said, every step dragging with hesitation.

*   *   *   *   *

On board the Flying Fitz

The cabin of the small plane was a cozy two-seater. Yes, Richard told his mother, she would need to use the headphones so they could hear each other over the engine noise. No, she would not need to use the controls in front of her. He started the engine.

"Dickie, your airplane reminds me for all the world of your father's Nash Metropolitan. He loved that automobile. Do you remember that? You were small enough then that we could put you in that miniscule back seat." Richard turned to his mother and adjusted her headset to hear her reedy words.

Sheila continued, "He loved that car, even though it killed him. But after my years of quixotic legal battles, the insurance lawyers finally said that 'pronounced understeering' and 'the unnecessarily high position of the steering wheel' made him lose control as he turned onto the bridge over the Charles River dam."

Richard listened to his mother, then spoke with the control tower for clearance and with departure control. His voice was tinny in the headphones. He said "Sorry, Mom, wasn't ignoring you. Just need to get ready for our flight. I was listening, though." *But, Mom, do you know you've told me this already?*

"Are you ready for takeoff, Mom?"

"Well," came her voice, tiny in the headphones, "yes. And *no*. But let's go."

"Hold on, then! As the kids say, it's a rush!"

Sheila gripped her son's arm as the *Flying Fitz* bounced along the runway, the buzz of the engine sounding louder and louder. The small plane sang a steady note as it leaped up to unzip the sky.

The throbbing engine made the day into a song without words. A bright sky flew over bare baby hills: no green fuses drove flowers or grass, just slow waves of earth, like a blanket not quite smoothed out.

"Mars! It looks exactly as I picture Mars." Mrs. Short leaned against the plane's window as she spoke into the headset's microphone. "Don't you miss all those nice trees in Washington? I'd certainly pine away without my palm trees," she said and laughed at her own joke.

Richard said, "That's because we're flying so low, well under 1,000 feet Mom, a bit low for Mars. I don't want the change in altitude to be too much for you." *I hope not too high for you to be able to breathe.* He leaned forward and gave the gauges a flick, paying special attention to the manifold pressure to check for engine bog. He kept one ear free of his headphones to listen for the sound of the plane's exhaust: too much pitch, engine too rich.

"Oh, Mom, before I forget to tell you, we'll be seeing Kevin and Randa while you're here. Did I tell you he's retiring? He's retiring today. Tonight really, right after graduation." Richard kept his eyes in motion, slowly moving them left and right, checking the Martian landscape and the crayon-blue sky.

The engine sputtered for a moment. Richard patted his mother's shoulder to reassure her. "Not to worry, Mom, it's just a cranky carburetor. We'll be at the Pancho Barnes Airpark soon." He shrugged as if to say sorry, unavoidable.

"Wonderful, Dickie. I'm not really provisioned for a jornada."

He looked at her with question-mark eyes, afraid to learn even one more word from his mother. "*Jornada*, Mom?"

"Yes, dear, it means a full day's travel across a desert— like that below us—without stopping to take on water. I hope that's not too recherché, is it dear? After all, I don't want to have a monosyllabic son, do I?"

"No, Mom."

He checked the RPMs on the instrument panel, trying to anticipate anything—everything, he told his mother—and give his altimeter a flick. He lifted his eyes to check the sky around them. He lifted his headphone to check his mother's thin breathing. Reassured, he let it snap back into place. The plane lifted them higher as he pulled back on the yoke.

"Yes, Dickie, it certainly looks like Mars."

*   *   *   *   *

Homes Again, again

Eloise Tristler reached across her desk to answer the telephone. Again. She was certain it would be Randa D'Arcangelo. *Yes and No*, she muttered to herself. "Homes Again, how may I help you?" *Bet I can guess: You want carrara marble instead of those antique tin tiles, a prep island, pops of color, soft-close drawers, waterfall countertops, architectural detail on your pergola, coffered ceilings, a rustic vibe, dark wood floors, dark kitchen cabinets...and all the other hoo-has you see on TV. But... her business has kept Homes Again afloat, not easy to do in a town this size. Guess she's the right one in ten-thousand...*

"Oh, hello again Homes Again!" Randa laughed at her own joke. Eloise sighed.

"What can I do for you, Mrs. D'Arcangelo?"

"This isn't about work, so please relax Eloise. It's about Loopers." Eloise cringed.

"Please, Mrs. D'Arcangelo, please don't call it that. It mocks our sincerity. We like to call it 'The Society' or by its full name. But, anyway, what can I do for you?"

"Okay. I'm calling to let you know the headphones have come in. They shipped them to me by mistake. Want to meet me at the Society when you're finished work? I'll bring them and you can show me how the training works. I can't wait!"

At last, our headphones! The last piece is in place. "Yes, yes, yes please! Oh, and Mrs. D'Arcangelo, just for fun, let's call it *entrainment*. Or synchronizing if you must, okay?"

"Oh, sure, Eloise. I've been getting ready for the next step, doing my meditation every day. See you about five, then?"

"Why wait? I can be there in about fifteen minutes. Have a day!" Eloise hung up without waiting for an answer, and almost danced down the hall to the back room of her office. She opened the storage closet, loaded audio equipment from its shelves on to a wheeled cart, and rolled the full cart out the back door to her Prius. *Had a feeling this was going to happen soon. Good thing I got everything organized.*

Eloise heard a dull thrum as she started her car and pulled out on to Boy Street. It was straight and empty under the noon sun. Houses and trees tucked their shadows under them. In her rearview mirror she saw that Boulder was no bigger than a thumbnail. She was alone on the street, but surrounded by a growing rumble. A shadow dragged across the road in front of her.

Eloise lowered all the windows in her car, and leaned out to listen more closely. *I'll bet my last batch of shiplap that's a B flat. Oh, those damn planes! When I become mayor, first thing I'll do is cancel some flying permits.*

Eloise leaned back in her SofTex®-trimmed seat, took a deep breath, and tightened her diaphragm. Her lips lightly parted, she hummed along with the airplane's engine. She sang a third higher, then a perfect fifth above the plane's B-flat, giving it a slow, warm vibrato. Her skin tingled. She belted out a major seventh, bent the pitch upward, and resolved it into an octave. *Ah, that was so nice.*

Eloise Tristler was gone as she sang, feeling a vibration that left her without life or death, beginning or ending, sorrow or joy, a sound that was its own sense. Her voice ebbed as the plane few away, taking its engine noise with it.

At the sign for the Mobius Metaphysical Meditation Society, she raised the car windows, turned on her blinker, and prepared to act as if nothing happened. "Head back in the game, Eloise," she said to herself. "But *that's* how I wish I sang for my Julliard audition."

Above Eloise, aboard the Flying Fitz, Sheila tapped on her window. "Dickie, Dickie, what is that strange building down there? The one by that big bare patch. Shall we detour and reconnoiter?"

"Sure, Mom."

The Flying Fitz pulled the earth even closer.

*   *   *   *   *

*Broken Bone Junior High School,
On the roof*

As Aria and Kevin burst over the ladder, they could see a day moon through isinglass clouds. The blue sky ate their eyes, the breeze poured syllables into their ears. The final school bells rang, metallic circles dissolving into the air. Below, school children fled—dots and dashes. Warm wind and soft hushes took their places. The clear sky spread a listening silence with a large trowel.

The broad, flat roof of Broken Bone Junior High School was a two-dimensional jungle of rusty red shingles. The roof dropped and rose over different sections of the school, each section taking its own place in a horizontal scale. The band room roof swung out from the school in a long, slow arc. The Math and Science wing took shelter under a right-angled canopy: sideways stairs. The gymnasium roof was a right hook. Squat turbine shafts, like aluminum lunar landers, spun and squeaked. Seen from above, the roof was an aircraft carrier beside Lake No One, a lake in dry dock that ran along the school's track.

Kevin hunched and rubbed his knee caps. "*Man*, it's so quiet up here, you could hear a fish blink! What a wild roof. This looks like an old Escher poster! Once a hippie always a hippie, I always say... "

"Good old *orthogonality* will do it every time. I always say! Or at least to those who throw words like anacrusis at me." Aria leaned against the elevator shaft's wall and lit her cigarette. Wind fingers discomposed her sunny hair; blonde hair on blue heaven. "But," she said after her first deep drag, "at least you can explain off better than most. Maybe it's the Professor Harold Hill in you."

"As Richard's mother would say, 'Those who can, teach.' And now I don't. Not sure what she would make of that."

"As your kooky wife would say, 'Yes and No'—whatever that means."

"Ah, Randa, Randa, my sweet Veranda! Can't remember when she started making all these wrong turns in her head. Could be it was her motorcycle accident, with those headaches, those bad moods. But I'd like to blame it on that new church, the one that took over the store front law firm that closed a while back on Every Street. O'Johns and Richards, I think. Or maybe it was Broken Bone Estates, they come and go, maybe they're even the same thing. Know anything about it? The new age group that moved in there, I mean. Randa just talks in circles when I ask her."

"Yes, without a No. That's the Mobius Metaphysical Meditation Society. Loopers, some folks call them."

"Loopers? Sounds like a good name. Randa's definitely that. That goofy decorator got her started with them."

"I feel bad for Randa."

"Feel bad for," Kevin said, swatting at his ear, "us." He swatted at his ear again. "You didn't tell me we had bees up here on the roof. Sounds like a *giant* bee too."

Aria finished her cigarette and flicked it over the edge. "Henry Hill, we got trouble, right here in Broken Bone city. Let me tell you about the Loopers." She took a step toward him, facing him squarely. "First, take off your belt."

"*What?* Aria, you're practically my niece. Kind of, sort of, but still... I'm happily married to a lunatic, and all that."

"Never mind that. Take off your belt." The wind dropped to the ground as Kevin removed his belt. He held his belt loop with one hand, his belt in the other.

"Okay, *uncle* Kevin, give it half a twist then buckle it again."

"But—"

"Don't argue. Remember, I'm a teacher too. Oh: and you aren't a teacher anymore. Anyway, no argument." He did as she demanded, struggling to keep his pants up at the same time.

"Now, use your finger to trace all the way around your belt. Remember, teacher said *all* the way. Tell me what happens." Again, he followed her command.

"Wait, are you sure? I don't, I mean *man*, I mean let me think about this. Oh, this is just weird." He traced around the belt again with this finger. "Starts on the outside and then goes to the inside and back again. Heavy, as we used to say. But can I put my belt back on yet, *teach?*"

"Not quite yet. Today's lesson is that the belt had two sides. Now, thanks to Mobius, a mathematician, it has only one side. With me so far?" He looked at his belt again.

"Um, yeah, but—" The bass note was getting louder, but he didn't have a free swatting hand.

Aria raised her voice over the growing buzz. "Loopers believe this proves there is only one side to reality. Yes and No are not opposites, they're the same. Quite a leap, yes?

And that's just the beginning. Wait until I tell you about their meditation, and then the binaural beats."

"Yes, but—" The thrum was loud enough to drown out his words. A shadow passed over them; startled, he looked up and let go of his belt and pants. He saw a small plane flying low, flying slow, almost hovering over the school as it dipped its wings, close and slow enough to read the sign on the bottom of the plane: it was The Flying Sheila Fitzgerald Short! The Flying Fitz accelerated up a spiral, Kevin's pants sank to the roof.

"Ginger peachy. Looks like your pants could use a little anacrusis. Bet you weren't prepared for that! And it looks like your old buddy Richard Short caught you with your pants down, eh *uncle?*"

Kevin's toothy smile at her little jokes was far from his eyes.

She winked one eye and then the other. "Better get ready to explain off to Randa. And every man jack in Broken Bone." She started toward the ladder, then turned to face him.

She said softly, "Chances are, he never got over losing Randa to you. Yes and no? So, Professor Hill, it looks like it's time to get ready..." The wind rose again, sounds with no sense.

* * * * *

Broken Bone Junior High School,
Above the roof

Mrs. Short leaned back from the airplane window and said "Dickie darling, who was that man down there, that man who looks like Randolph Mantooth?" She was nearly breathless. "And in a distracting state of deshabillé!"

"That word means with his pants down, right? Well, Mom, you asked me what happened to Kevin, my colleague who went missing. That was Kevin. I guess he's preparing to celebrate his retirement. But that just didn't look like Randa." *He never will let me forget she was mine once.*

"Please ascend, Dickie. Lawks-a-mussy." The engine noise covered the sound of her inhaler.

"Mom, we're going to land at an airpark named after Pancho Barnes. Have you heard of her?"

"What did she write? And is that the correct pronoun?"

"She—and she was a she—was a stunt pilot. Among other things. Raced against Amelia Earhart. Wild woman. Thought you would have heard of her in one of your women's courses. Her real name was Florence Lowe."

"She sounds provocative. Perhaps I can include her on next year's syllabus."

"And speaking of school, Mom, whatever happened to that grant money you applied for? You know, for all that Virginia Woolf stuff you teach?"

"They said my seminar on Virginia Woolf and her circle was *derivative.*" Sheila gave a small *humph.* "But they gave me the grant, regardless."

"Big wad of cash? Sorry to pry about money, Mom, just want to make sure you can get by is all."

"Yes, Dickie, big wad of cash. But... we're in it now."

Richard gave his mother a sidelong look, raising one eyebrow. "Elaborate, as you would say, Mom."

"We're *in* it." She flicked the door beside her, nearly catching her wristbands on the door handle. She crossed her ankles and sat quietly with her hands in her lap.

"But isn't—I thought you said the money—insurance, uncles..."

"Paltry sums. Paltry. Insulting, really."

Throat lumps choked Richard; he took the plane to a higher altitude to prepare for landing.

"And no need to worry about me, I have what I believe they call a sugar daddy waiting for me back in Florida." *Now that you didn't tell me before!*

Richard prepared their aircraft to land: bleeding off air speed, pulling back on the yolk, and—like a concert organist—worked his feet among the rudders to stop the Flying Fitz. He had no chance to respond to his mother's surprising announcement.

The Flying Fitz settled into a perfect landing at Pancho Barnes Airpark without another sound from its passengers.

*   *   *   *   *

Headquarters of Mobius Metaphysical Meditation Society, Broken Bone, Colorado

Eloise parked in the alley behind the Society's meeting hall. Gravel crunched as she backed her Prius within a few feet of its back door. She had parked, propped open the back door, and opened her hatchback by the time Randa arrived.

A pearly Cadillac Escalade pulled in beside Eloise's Black Sand Pearl car. Cool, scented air rushed out as the driver's door opened. Silver ballet slippers, pale pink yoga pants, and a pale pink tailored hoody: it was Randa. Her hoody was unzipped just enough to let her Japanese pearls catch the early afternoon sun.

"Eloise, how are you?" French *and* Italian, was that her accent? Eloise wondered. Never have been able to tell. I know the cycles per second of each and every syllable she utters, but still can't pin down her accent.

"Hippy skippy, Mrs. D'Arcangelo. Glad you called me, I've been wondering where the sam fat those headphones got to." Eloise spoke to Randa as she opened the back door continued to unload her car. "Hope you brought them with you."

"Oh, yes, Eloise. Would you like me to take them in for you?"

Well, duh. "Yes, please." Eloise struggled with the heavy electronic equipment as Randa toted a shopping bag of headphones into the Society's meeting room.

Randa set the bag down just inside the door, then stepped through the curtain that separated the back room from the main meeting space. "Eloise, you are really a miracle worker. Really. Who else could take this dusty old office and turn it into a glamorous meeting place?" Randa swept her arms around the large room; her pearls swung free with a clear and glassy sound. "Gorgeous hard wood floors, original, yes? Trendy shiplap walls, open-concept to the max, and those amazing customized theater seats. It must have cost you a *fortune* to get them to curve like that, each row up on a riser."

In the center of the room, twenty theater seats formed a semicircle. Each seat had plush cushions of memory foam, and a footrest that popped out when the seat reclined. Polished cherry wood arms had cup holders and jacks for headphones.

"And how ever did you find someone to set them up for our headphones?"

Well, you're the one who paid me a fortune, so that should answer your question. But that's why I drive such a dinky car. "Oh, money talks, though with me it's barely a whisper. But it's all for a good cause, Mrs. D'Arcangelo." Eloise arranged the electronic equipment on the shelves she had made for it, and began plugging in the components. She held the curtain open and asked "Mind helping with the headphones? Just take them out of their boxes, and plug them into the jacks at each seat. We can store the boxes back here."

As Randa distributed the headphones, Eloise stood at the podium and turned on the large monitor. She used the podium's keyboard to connect all the equipment, and told Randa they were done.

"My," Randa said, "that seems simple. Is that all there is to it?" She sat down in the front row and slid out a foot rest.

Simple. Sure. Three years of planning and who knows *how much of my own money. It's just that simple.* "Yup. Want to take it for a test drive?"

Randa picked up a set of headphones, she said "Oh, one thing. Before we start, can you please explain it to me again?"

With deliberate movements, Eloise forced a few commands into her computer keyboard. A slide show started behind her on the large screen. She picked up a laser pointer, and spoke as if she were on an infomercial.

"First, we have the philosophy of Yes and No. The belt here *seems* to have two sides. We use it to represent reality. But Mobius tells us there is really one side when you give the belt—reality—a half-twist. Watch as I trace the laser around this picture. So life isn't Yes *or* No, it's both."

Randa sat quietly for a few moments, then raised her hand. Eloise sighed. "Yes, ma'am, you in the front row?"

Across her smooth brow, in the area between her perfect eyebrows, in the land of concentration, a small wrinkle appeared. "I just had a mental thought! I *get* it! So *that's* what you've been saying, Yes *and* No. Oh, I get it, I get it!!!" Eloise saw a light in Randa's face she had not seen before.

"Yes, ma'am. Yes and No, I should say. Now, this—," she advanced the show to the next slide—, "shows us the meditation technique. We use this to help us see the half-twist in reality."

Randa started to speak again, but Eloise continued. "It's simple. Sit quietly. Close your eyes, and move them slowly from side to side. Slow eye movements imitate REM sleep, making you feel calm and peaceful." Eloise's laser highlighted the bullet points on the screen behind her. "Feel free to breathe in and out as you move your eyes. Do this for about thirty minutes each day."

Randa began to follow Eloise's words. Eloise could see her chest rising in slow, even movements. "You can, if you wish, sigh or moan as you let your breath out. It helps some people."

A breathy sound came from Randa's throat.

"Our third step is to help our brains retain these insights. That's why we use binaural beats. As you get ready to meditate, put on the headphones and play our CD. You will hear a steady tone, a slightly different tone in each ear. Your brain creates a third tone and turns the tone into a wave that feels peaceful. We call this *entrainment*. Just when your ears hear this wave, your brain makes you feel calm and relaxed."

Eloise gave a broad smile to her imaginary infomercial camera. "See? No thought required at all!" *And I know someone who will benefit from that…*

Eloise stepped beside Randa. She said, "Randa, you can keep your eyes closed. I'll hand you your headphones. Put them on and press the round button on your armrest. It will turn off after about 30 minutes. Keep breathing and moving your eyes, slowly, until the sounds stop."

Randa slipped on the headphones and pressed the round button. Eloise saw her eyes move left and right, tone-driven pendulums. She slipped into the seat next to hers, and started her own journey to peace. The song in her headphones was a sound that was its own sense.

* * * * *

Broken Bone Junior High School Auditorium,
Commencement, 8:45 p.m.

Kevin D'Arcangelo urged his musicians to keep playing *Pomp and Circumstance* in a never-ending loop. Adolescents tripped across the stage, a little further along the path to adulthood and higher education. Proud parents sat on thin-cushioned chairs and applauded their offspring.

When the Principal, Victoria Welden, called Gwen's name, the band stopped playing. She left her flute on her chair and climbed the stage to accept the paper. The entire band rubbed their feet across the floor, a musician's way to applaud without letting go of their instruments. In the front row, her parents—Marshall and Sandro—gave the air a punch.

At the end of the ceremony, Principal Welden announced this was also a farewell to their beloved music teacher, Kevin D'Arcangelo.

"No, no, that came out wrong," said Ms Welden. "I meant that Kevin is retiring, nothing more sinister! There's punch and cookies to celebrate both happy occasions at the back of the room. Please help yourselves."

The children chattered in corners and adults collected around the punch and cookies table. Broken Bone's founders, Dr. Zachary Ritenour and Octavia, looked at the gathering through their painted portrait eyes, as pleased as painted portraits could look pleased. Kevin stood at the end of the table, shaking hands and smiling, and looking for his wife. He spotted Richard standing in a small group near the table and waved to get his attention.

"Richard, have you seen Randa?" he asked his friend as he walked over. "She said she'd drop by after she ran an errand, and that was *hours* ago. I know she likes to make an appearance, but this is much, even for her."

Before he could reply, he heard a voice from out of his past, unmistakable in its crisp diction and imperious delivery: it was Sheila Fitzgerald Short. "Dickie, darling, have you … oh, *there* you are, Kevin dear. You young men move away from that table so we can have a salubrious confab." She smoothed a wrinkle from her periwinkle velour dress, and adjusted the tilt of her aubergine fascinator.

"Yes, Mom," and "Yes, Mrs. Short." Like overdressed ants, they filed into the last row of seats in the auditorium, well away from the noise, cake, soda, balloons, and exuberant graduates: Richard, his mother, Kevin.

"Kevin, before I forget, you must thank your father for all those nice key limes he sent me. I find them so *indispensable*. How very thoughtful. I hope the Ambassador and your mother are enjoying retirement in their new California home."

Not waiting for an answer, she asked, "And what of your lovely wife? Richard has told me so many nice things about her. Very Audrey Hepburn, from what I gather." She reached in her clutch and retrieved her inhaler. Richard noticed it had a gold lamé case, engraved with her initials.

"Yes, Mrs. Short, she's very special. But missing, at the moment. I don't want to be rude, but if there isn't anything special you want to discuss, I'm expected back at—"

"Oh, but there is young man. And *I* don't want to be rude. It seems my son and I saw something today, something I'm uncomfortable sharing with you."

Richard slouched, and crossed his arms. "Mom, I don't think we should—"

Sheila turned to her son, the feathers and veil on her fascinator rippling as she turned. "Tosh and tutty-kins, Dickie. Kevin," she said, turning to look at him, "we saw you on the roof today. You seem fascinated with the roof. But my point is you were in an embarrassing tête-à-tête with a woman, and must have forgotten to include your pants in the conversation!"

"I'm not sure about anything you said except pants, but," and he stood up in the aisle and looked down at them, "that woman is practically my niece. And, and, we were discussing Mobius and binaural beats. A purely academic discussion."

"But wait, man. Kevin. Wait a second. My mother and I were just saying—"

He turned his back and walked to the back doors of the auditorium.

Richard felt someone sit down beside him. He could smell fresh citrus as he turned to see a bright-headed woman next to him: It was Aria. She placed her hand on his wrist.

"Not to worry, Richard. Kevin will calm down. Especially," she leaned into him, unmistakably into him, "especially when he finds out about *us!*"

*　*　*　*　*

At the back of the auditorium, Kevin opened a back door as Randa walked in an adjacent door. He saw her and let his door close.

"Randa! I've been so worried. Are you alright?" His wife looked at him.

"Yes, yes, of course darling. But you look a bit excited." She took his arm and walked him to the punch and cookies table. "How about a nice Hawaiian Punch?" She offered him a paper cup of sweet red liquid from the table.

"In a moment. There's something I need to tell you," he said and stepped close enough to her so only she could hear. She took a step back and laughed.

"Oh, Kevin, Kevin dearest. I think I know. Broken Bone is *such* a small town." She rested a perfectly manicured hand on his chest. "You, Aria, the plane, the pants—or lack of them, really. Don't you know by now I trust you *completely?*"

He leaned back against the end of the table and pulled her to him again, closer than before. "Randa, Randa, my Veranda." They both smiled. "Yes, words do fly around here. Some true, some not. But... does this have anything to do with why you're so late? You know my motto about preparation, and follow through."

"Yes, dear," she mocked. "And No. Yes and No." She laughed, and reached into her purse.

"Yes and no? You know I just don't understand you some—"

"Yes, dear, and no again. I mean the silly rumor has nothing to do with why I am late. I feel better than I have in years. That motorcycle accident, my headaches, my bad moods—I'm much better now. But what I'm trying to tell you is that I got my royalty check in the mail."

She kissed him on the cheek. "Darling, remember all those celebrity voice-overs I did last year? Who would have thought people would think I actually sound like Audrey Hepburn. Anyway, darling, I'm going to treat you, us, to a retirement trip around the world."

"But, but... but Randa!"

"Not to worry, my darling. The check is huge!" She widened her Audrey Hepburn eyes at him. "Simply *huge*, darling," she said in her best imitation of the star, "simply *huge*."

"And one more thing, husband." She took his elbow and led him out the door. "Don't worry, dear. You *can* fly. I'll show you how. It's all in how you cup your hands. That's the secret."

Maybe

Vinca Terrace, St. Petersburg, Florida, August, 2015

Sheila Fitzgerald Short pulled lightly at the Heavenly Blue Morning Glories that crocheted themselves across the screen of her balcony, reaching up. "Enough of this tortuosity," she said to the vines, "it's quite unbecoming to be so twisted. Would it be unnatural for you to grow in straight lines?" The flowers shook in the hot, heavy breeze that rubbed against animate and inanimate objects alike. Four floors below, laying across grass and asphalt, shadows dripped in a slow sizzle. Another summer storm was likely but, Sheila thought, unnecessary.

"Lawks-a-mussy," she said aloud as she worked to separate the vines, "this weather keeps me in a constant state of inelegance." Tired, she sat down in her swivel chair and sipped on barley-water and brandy. Sheila had nearly dozed off when she heard the balcony's glass doors slide open.

"Sheila-kins, are you awake dear?" Celeste, her life-long friend, stood in the balcony doorway "Perhaps you should come in out of the heat, sweetie. It's deliciously cool in here."

Wordlessly, Celeste helped her frail friend out of her chair and into the cave-cool interior. They sat, side-by-side, on Sheila's rattan couch. After a few moments, Celeste patted her friend's hand and asked if she wanted a cool drink, or something to eat.

"After all," Celeste said as she moved into the kitchen before Sheila could answer, "after all, those nice people from *Air Today* will be here soon."

"Botheration," said Sheila as she took a cool drink from her friend. "I simply don't know why Dr. Hagopian wants them to bring me oxygen. You know I'm not valetudinarian enough to deserve that."

Celeste, sitting in an armchair by the couch, blinked. "Sheila, we've been friends a *very, very* long time, have we not?"

"Of course, Celeste. Why, you've been my friend, my diary, since we were young girls!" She paused to catch her breath. "Is something wrong, dear? With you, I mean, or Joseph?"

Celeste laughed. "No, Sheila, not at all! It's just that— well, I don't know how to say it—I'm not certain what that word means! And—"

Before Sheila could reply, she continued, "—and, I know you always took first place in our vocabulary contests, and I was second, always, but ... well, I'm trying to say I don't always understand you!"

Sheila laughed, then bent double in a cough. When she recovered, she said, "Celeste, sweetie. I was just trying to say I'm too healthy for that oxygen tank they want me to use! Of course," she continued, mostly to herself, "valetudinarian can mean a person who is unduly anxious about their health. Or it can mean a person, unlike me, who is suffering from poor health. The word comes from valetudo, *state of health*, which comes from valere. You know: *be strong*. I feel strong."

Celeste patted the air with a "settle down" gesture. "Yes, sweetie. But I have a question."

Sheila grew attentive.

"Do words mean something if no one looks them up?"

Sheila sat back in the couch. "Well," she said, drawing a deep, delicate breath, "well, it's a matter of perspective, of where we direct our attention. But I'm not as perspicacious as I would like to be. And I always say, the only way out of this oubliette is up. Maybe that's why my flowers climb? Or perhaps life is more like a calaboose, I'm not certain."

Celeste shrugged, then rose. "Must dash, Sheila-kins. Joseph wants leg of lamb tonight. That man is made of meat, I believe. My little meaty-kins. Tooda-loo! I'll call you later!" She left, leaving the inner door open to let in the day.

A nap nipped at Sheila, grazing on her thoughts. Muffled sounds from the walkway intruded.

That's either Tiffany for a hat fitting, or those pesky air people, Sheila thought. She wafted down her front hall and squinted through the screen door. "Yes?" she asked the man and woman standing on the walkway. The sun, rising over the bay behind them, condensed them to shady essences. *Odd looking day out there,* thought Sheila, *not your usual sun-sky-water decoupage.* The bay water was the color of the August sky, each cloud an indistinct barge.

"Mrs. Short?" asked the middle-aged, bearded man. He wore pale blue medical scrubs, and held the handle of an oxygen concentrator that looked like drag-behind luggage on wheels. Beside him, a short, red-haired woman wore rose-colored medical scrubs and carried a clipboard and a purse. "I'm Donnie, Donnie D'Arcangelo, this is Elizabeth Ritenour. We're from *Air Today*. May we come in?"

Silently, Sheila opened her screen door. "Why the heck and why not anyways?" she asked. She gestured to the couch and asked "Tea? Hibiscus. Good for the blood pressure, I'm told. And if you're peckish, I've made some Garnet and Gold cupcakes, my salute to the Florida flag."

Donnie and Elizabeth exchanged glances as they sank into Sheila Short's sofa cushions. "Oh, no thanks," said Elizabeth, her deep contralto voice contrasting with her petite frame. "I brought water, and we're not much for sugar. Thanks just the same." Elizabeth lifted a large bottle of water from her over-sized purse, and took a swig.

"Well," said Sheila, sitting upright in her rattan chair, her hands overlapping each other, "well, what can I do for you today?"

Donnie and Elizabeth looked intently at Sheila. "Do tell us a little about yourself, Mrs. Short. Elizabeth will take notes, if you don't mind."

"Yes. I mean no, I don't mind." Sheila leaned back in her chair, feeling lightheaded. "But first, I'd like to turn off the air conditioning. I'm feeling quite algid."

"Bingo!" yelled Donnie and jumped up. "Mrs. Short, you're spectacular! Algid. *Algid.* That's beyond all our hopes, our expectations." Elizabeth tugged on the sleeve of his scrubs and gently pulled him back into his seat.

"What? *What?!* I am nonplussed. More than usual."

"Mrs. Short," Elizabeth said in a soothing voice, "we are here to help you."

"All too tautological." Sheila began to see flashes of lightning in the corner of her eyes, a precursor to a migraine.

Donnie said "Bingo!" again in a more subdued voice. He turned to Elizabeth, his eyes shining. "We should tell her everything."

Elizabeth frowned. She looked down and said, "What would Diane say? We won't be sending another report for ten days, the Library will be closed for Independence Day." She turned and looked at Donnie, her face a map of confusion and frustration. "Yes, we must tell her, but what would Diane say?"

"Excuse me!" Sheila's voice was feeble, but carried command. "Excuse me!" She struggled to stand, and looked for her inhaler. "Explain yourselves now or leave. Preferably both." She waved a hand at the door.

"Oh, dear, Mrs. Short, I'm afraid we've gone about this all wrong," Elizabeth said. "All wrong. But before we do anything, we must give you some oxygen. Donnie brought the latest in air concentrators, the Philips Respironics

EverFlo Q. I can tell you're nearing a crisis, we can't wait too much longer to help you. Why, you're as pale as gadolinium!" Elizabeth's eyes pleaded.

Sheila sat down on the edge of her chair. "Crisis? I thought you were just going to give me an oxygen treatment then get out of my life." She closed her eyes; the lightning flashes were still visible, and other geometric shapes were pulsing on the inside of her eyelids.

Donnie stood up, set his cheery yellow concentrator beside Sheila, and squatted alongside her chair. He slipped a pulse oximeter on her forefinger. It beeped a few seconds later; he checked its readings and removed it. With a dab hand, he placed a mask over Sheila's nose and mouth and started the machine. Her wrist was cool to his touch as he took her pulse, the blue veins visible through her isinglass skin.

"Are we in time, Donnie?"

"Yes."

"Not too soon, either?" She raised an eyebrow.

"No. We're not too soon, Liz. Maybe ... maybe we timed it just right."

"While we're waiting for oxygen to help you," Elizabeth said, taking Mrs. Short's other hand in hers, "let me tell you what this is all about." She sat, cross-legged, at Sheila's feet.

* * * * *

The Anacrusis

"Before this story began," began Elizabeth, "there was a great *anacrusis*, a preparation, in what is known as the Bubble Galaxy. There was a mighty explosion, a supernova, six light-years wide. That explosion forced a planet, OTS 44, out of its solar system. Our story begins with that planet, that *rogue* planet."

Donnie adjusted Sheila's oxygen flow, and she stirred.

Elizabeth continued. "OTS 44 is big, at least a dozen times the mass of Jupiter. Some believe it will become its own planetary system. And, just like in a hokey science fiction movie, it's headed directly for Earth. That's where *we* come into the story."

Elizabeth rubbed Sheila's hands between hers to warm them. Sheila's eyelids flickered briefly.

"We are from Planet 77 in the Galaxy 88. Not their real names, of course, but names are meaningless when the planets and galaxies are so far away. Names are, in their own way, as horrible as division by zero." Donnie gave a small cough, as if to say stick to the subject. Elizabeth continued, standing and rubbing Sheila's forearms as she spoke.

"We are called Guiders. We help prepare those whose homes are destined to be destroyed. To make it stick-figure simple, we have been working through people on Earth to prepare them for the inevitable collision." Sheila's eyes moved slowly back and forth beneath her eyelids; she moaned. Donnie increased the flow of air. The concentrator emitted two low hums.

"Starting back in your year 1872, we guided Dr. Zachary Ritenour and his wife, Octavia, to set up a home base. They called it Broken Bone. We used magnetos and magic, as they say, to alter their brains so their vocabulary affects those around them. For them, and for you, the changes happen below your awareness: flashes of sounds, faint smells. The changes take only nanoseconds, but they have a huge effect on your feelings and behaviors. Actually," Elizabeth said, her hands fluttering in the air for emphasis, speaking with quick enthusiasm, "we take readings from the spectra of hydrated manganese chloride crystals, refined by means of three-dimensional differential syntheses, then match this with—"

Donnie gave a louder, more distinct editorial cough.

"Sorry, I digress. Anyway, some call this altered vocabulary Neuro Linguistic Programming, NLP, but it is not well understood here, and has been discredited. Mostly through our disinformation efforts. NLP is a form of verbal suasion, encouraging your essence—some call it your soul—to prepare itself and, just before your catastrophe, migrate to the Well of Souls. From there, your essences *twist* to a trans-dimensional ship. That ship will tour the galaxies until you find a suitable location to inhabit."

"Pssst..." said Donnie, "she's going to be fully awake soon. Please, please get to the point!"

Elizabeth waved her hand in a "shush" motion. She gently placed Sheila's arms on the rests of her chair. "Anywho, we want you to know that you are special, along with your friend Barry." Sheila's lips parted, but she did not speak.

"Yes, you and Barry, among others, transmit *our* anacrusis, our preparatory steps, when you speak to others. No one, of course, knows this is happening. We want to keep you healthy and happy until your time comes to leave this oubliette."

"Sheila, can you hear me?" Donnie spoke softly into Sheila's ear. He increased the air flow on the concentrator.

"Oh, and one more thing," said Elizabeth. "We have many Reporters, as we call them. People who report back to our leader, Diane. They don't know they are reporting, but feel a need to gather together, which is necessary to send their reports to Diane. We find that writers are good observers, so we choose many of them as Reporters."

Donnie and Elizabeth stepped back to look at Sheila; the hiss of the concentrator filled the room.

"What... what is ...soo... soo...," Sheila faltered, took a deep breath, and said, slowly and distinctly and imperiously, "Just what *is* that susurration?" Her eyes fluttered, then stayed opened.

Donnie stood, then took a pamphlet and a book out of his pocket. "Mrs. Short, we know you may feel a little disoriented now, maybe for a few hours, and will probably sleep for a while. We'll be back again, probably next week. You should start to feel better as soon as you wake up."

Sheila fell asleep as she saw Donnie and Elizabeth, indistinct silhouettes, slip out her screen door.

*   *   *   *   *

Two hours later

Tiffany looked at Celeste, then down at Sheila, stretched out on her rattan couch. "She looks okey-dokey to me, Mrs. Lobosco. Sleeping like a baby. Thought you said she was real sick when you called."

"Sorry, I didn't mean to alarm you. I dropped by to invite Sheila to dinner. Her door was open, and she was like this, sleeping on her couch."

"Yeah no. She looks okay to me, from the looks of her." Tiffany reached down and gently touched Sheila's shoulder.

Sheila stirred and sat up, just as Barry Simmons walked through the door.

"Barry! Darling. You catch me in a state of deshabillé." Her eyes were shining, a flush of color in her cheeks. "But I believe that oxygen treatment did me a world of good." She stood up and smoothed her fuchsia culottes.

Celeste rolled her eyes. "Oh, Sheila," she said quietly, "I have a quick observation to share. Don't know how, so I'll just blurt it out."

"Yes? Well, whatever it is, you can—"

"Your culottes, Sheila. They're, I mean it's, I mean—well, you put *two* legs where just *one* would do. See" Celeste reached down and fanned out the empty leg of Sheila's culottes.

"Maybe," said Sheila, raising one eyebrow, "maybe the other one is just for emergencies?"

Barry took her hand and pulled her down onto the couch beside him.

Tiffany walked to the door saying, over her shoulder, "Mrs. Short, I'll see you next week with that new hat you wanted. Remember, that salute to Margaret Thatcher hat?" She waved goodbye through the screen door.

Celeste sat down. "Sheila, I was quite worried. I've never seen you sleep during the day, and you looked so, so ..."

"Rested?" Sheila offered. She smoothed the empty culotte to contour to her legs.

"Well, yes. Yes. Of course."

Barry stood. "Ah, yes. Well, if you don't mind a paraphrase of Romeo and Juliet, jocund day stands still stands on misty mountain tops. Or over the bay. Which means," he said, rising, "it means something like I think I left my refrigerator running, so I'll mosey home and give you two time to talk. I just dropped by to say hello, and that's done." He gave Sheila a bus on the forehead and headed out the door.

"Would you care for a bracing Vinca-tini, Celeste?"

Celeste rolled her eyes. "Oh, no, last time was more than enough, thank you. Though my nerves are unnerved, the way you looked while you were sleeping."

"Yes, a little less glamorously than I would hope for, *unencumbered by dignity or decorum,* as they say."

"Did those folks from *Air Today* drop by?"

Sheila frowned, and pulled her vestigial culotte leg taut, then looked up at Celeste. "I believe they did."

"They, Sheila? I don't know who you mean."

"Donnie and Elizabeth. I thought perhaps you saw them arrive as you left earlier. Ships passing in the day?"

"No, but that Vinca-tini is sounding appropriate right now. Is your offer still good?" Sheila nodded. "Please, I'll be glad to make my own. Care for one?" Sheila shook her head. Celeste headed for the tiki bar in the corner.

Back with another Vinca-tini, Celeste sat in the arm chair and emptied her beverage in one continuous motion. "Ah, that's good coffee, as they say. Good ole' Vinca-tini-kins. Long may they wave!" She gave a mock salute. "Care for another? Don't mind if I do. And how about you, Sheila?" Sheila smiled but said nothing, just waved toward the tiki bar.

As Celeste was mixing another beverage, Sheila said, "I *heard* them, in my dream. A sort of twilight sleep, they were talking to me. Something about planets and brain-washing, it's all quite indistinct now. Like flights of reason in those science fiction movies Dickie likes to watch. But the story seemed so retrodictable."

"Sheila, please? Your vocabulary is showing!" Celeste winked as she sat again.

"Sorry, dear. Predictable, but only after the fact. Like a detective story, where the criminal is obvious once the truth is unveiled, but not before. They implied that—"

The canary-yellow phone in Sheila's open-concept kitchen rang. Sheila waved to Celeste to stay in her seat as she moved to answer it.

"Yes, this is Mrs. Short," she said to the scratch-voiced caller. "Yes, that's my address," she answered the caller's question. "No, no, I've been here all day, I would have heard if someone—" and "Yes, *all* day. Why are you asking?" She listened, then said, "But they were here already, Donnie and Elizabeth."

Celeste slipped out onto the balcony, and plucked the strings of the vines like a guitar. A few moments later Sheila joined her.

"Curioser and curioser," she said to Celeste, and began to untwine the flowering vines again.

"What's that? It sounded like a very strange call." Celeste flopped down into the swivel chair.

"It was. Strange, that is. That was *Air Today*. They were apologizing, saying that Rose and Jim couldn't make it today." Sheila nodded her head toward the tiki bar. "Would you mind being mother, dear? One of those wonderful beverages sounds so salubrious right now. Feel free to make one for yourself, too."

As Celeste made their drinks, Sheila settled into the swivel chair, closed her eyes, and felt the warm breeze across her cheeks. "So strange," she thought, "all those dreams. As if I could hear stutters on the wall. Like *mental virga*, not quite reaching the ground. All this, I'm sure, would be so... *retrodictable* if only... if only I could fly!"

Mrs. Sheila Fitzgerald Short, recently of 417 Vinca Terrace, St. Petersburg, Florida, cupped her hands to catch the breeze from St. Pete Bay, and sailed up and out of her oubliette.

To My Readers

Thank you for taking the time to read *Broken Bone: Ten short, off-kilter stories*. I hope you enjoyed it. I had a lot of fun dreaming up adventures for my condo's residents, and how to sneak in a little of my own life as I went along.

If you enjoyed this book (or its companion book, *Vinca Terrace: A novel of comic condo consternation*), would you please take a moment to leave a review on Amazon and/or Goodreads? Reviews help us all decide what to read, but also help determine which books show up in search results.

I'm hard at work on the third book (I plan to call it *Return to Vinca*) in this series, so please keep checking those websites!

Thank you too much!

—Martin Crabtree

About the Author

Artwork by Rebecca Mashburn, 2019

Martin Crabtree, a native of Dorchester, Massachusetts, was a bassoonist, typesetter, and software trainer in Washington, D.C. Fearing for his sanity, he retired to Florida, where he holds a weak grip on reality. His lifelong philosophy is that *life makes no sense*, so we might as well develop a strong love of the absurd. He is author of the companion book to this novel, *Vinca Terrace: A Novel of Comic Condo Consternation,* and an upcoming third book in this series (tentatively titled *Return to Vinca*). He is planning to release another Vinca-Terrace book in the fall of 2019.

www.ingramcontent.com/pod-product-compliance
Lightning Source LLC
Chambersburg PA
CBHW030341180626
46812CB00007B/2717